T0031944

GUIDANCE TO DEATH

A NOVEL

DANIEL V. MEIER, JR.

North Carolina

Published in the United States by BQB Publishing
(an imprint of Boutique of Quality Books Publishing, Inc.)
www.bqbpublishing.com

979-8-88633-002-1 (p)
979-8-88633-003-8 (e)

Library of Congress Control Number: 2023934813

Book design by Robin Krauss, www.bookformatters.com
Cover design by Rebecca Lown, www.rebeccalowndesign.com
First editor: Caleb Guard
Second editor: Allison Itterly

PRAISE FOR
GUIDANCE TO DEATH
AND DANIEL V. MEIER, JR.

Daniel V. Meier, Jr.

". . . Satisfying twists and turns of plot keep even the most seasoned murder mystery reader guessing, while the aviation industry's processes and insights will delight those who enjoy tales of blackmail and threat that can take place in the unsafe skies and on the ground.

Murder mystery readers and libraries catering to them will find *Guidance to Death* an outstanding blend of action-packed thriller and whodunit. It is powered by the expertise of an author who is a retired FAA Aviation Safety Inspector able to inject all the real-world processes of the aviation industry into a compelling, can't-put-it-down inquiry that reaches its crescendo of surprise in the unfriendly skies."

– D. Donovan, Senior Reviewer, *Midwest Book Review* and Editor, *Donovan's Literary Services*

CHAPTER 1

1996
January 10
Saturday, 3:00 a.m.

T he weather was perfect: heavy clouds down to eight hundred feet, and a driving cold rain. Salvatore Sassavitte had been waiting for this day for over a month. An opportunity like this may not present itself for another month or more. The thing had to be done now. The longer it dragged on, the more likely he was to do something extremely careless.

The tie he was wearing bit into his throat. He loosened it slightly. A dark, ghostly image of himself reflected in the windshield of the van. He had never worn a suit to work before. This was the first time, and he promised himself it would be the last.

He double-checked his tools and stowed them in his black attaché case. He stepped quietly out of his van, slipped on his black wool overcoat, and walked briskly across the executive parking lot toward the secure area with his attaché case in hand.

The guard on the gate, sleepy from a long shift in his overheated guard house, nodded indifferently as Salvatore flashed a company identification card and airport ramp pass. The guard would not remember it. To him, Salvatore was probably just another Washington lawyer. They came and went through this gate at all hours of the day and night, and at three o'clock on a cold January morning, nobody cared.

He walked across the wet, icy ramp to the silent jet, opened the cabin door, lowered the entry stairs, and stepped into its snug, carpeted interior. He would have to work fast. The plane would be departing in a few hours, and the task ahead of him was not an easy one. "Mustn't fumble the precision tools in the dark, cold cockpit," he said to himself. Sal had researched it thoroughly and rehearsed the procedures until he was sure he had accounted for every eventuality. No room for mistakes or complications. He blew into his cupped hands for warmth, then opened the attaché case. He turned on his small flashlight and placed it in his mouth, pointing the shaft of light at the instrument panel, and started working.

After an hour and a half of work, he retightened the last fastener on the integrated guidance system. Then he hurriedly closed the plane up, careful to leave no trace. He then walked back, past another dozing guard and out of the gate. Once he was in his van, he drove to a small public park near the north end of the longest runway.

Sal kept the engine running with the defroster on full heat. He wanted to have a clear view of the runway when the time came. He sat with his feet up against the dash, sipping a blend of coffee and brandy from a thermos. He switched on his portable multi-band radio and tuned it to the airport's ground control frequency. He tried to fight the urge to sleep, but at some point, his eyelids closed, and he was out.

He was startled awake by the sharp, clear sound of his radio. It was 7:30, and a pilot was calling for a departure clearance under instrument flight rules. It was a voice he recognized. He had listened to that voice a few times at company parties. It was a good voice, belonging to an average guy like himself, a guy who was just trying to make a living doing what he liked best. "That's too bad," Sal muttered to himself, "but there's no other way. Sacrifices have to be made if you want to advance in this world."

The clearance came through loud and clear. Sal picked up his binoculars and scanned the ramp until he saw the jet's red and green navigation lights moving slowly toward him, rocking on its nose wheel, strobe lights flashing. He watched as the jet moved down the long taxiway to the end of the runway. He could hear the faint whine of the engines as the pilot ran his final cockpit checks. Sal switched to the tower frequency and heard the voice from the tower, "Cleared for takeoff."

The jet moved into position on Runway 19 and accelerated down the centerline of the black runway, leaving two swirling trails of dark exhaust behind. He followed the plane as it climbed out of a cloud of hot steam created by the jet blast on the wet runway. He continued to watch as the jet was swallowed up, with surprising quickness, by the black-gray layer of stratus cloud hovering several hundred feet above Reagan National Airport and the city of Washington, DC. He hurriedly switched to the jet's assigned departure control frequency.

"Citation 99 Alpha are you receiving me?" the controller's voice demanded.

"Affirmative," answered the pilot, betraying no alarm.

"Citation 99 Alpha, radar shows you at seven thousand feet."

"Standby," answered the pilot calmly.

"Citation 99 Alpha, can you climb and maintain flight level 180?"

"Standby," answered the pilot, still professionally calm.

A few seconds passed.

"Citation 99 Alpha, we've lost you on radar. Are you receiving me? Can you read me?"

No answer. The controller tried again.

"Citation 99 Alpha, are you receiving me? Are you receiving me? If you are receiving me, squawk ident."

Sal switched off the radio, put the van in gear, and drove out of the small park onto a nearly deserted George Washington Parkway. He smiled as he drove home. He and his wife were leaving for the Virgin Islands in a couple of hours, leaving a freezing capital and its crime-infested streets forever.

Kevin Oakes was driving the last leg of his paper route and running slightly later than usual. Several blocks away, he noticed a car parked in front of the Campbell house, his most difficult customer. If Mr. Campbell wasn't complaining about the price of the paper, he complained about its contents, and he never forgot to remind Kevin of the days he had been late. Mr. Campbell even showed him a calendar where he had marked it all down and had even refused to pay for several copies, claiming that he did not have time to read them until late in the afternoon, after work, when the news was old and useless.

Kevin did not feel like a confrontation this morning. He'd sooner give up the route entirely and find another job where he did not have to deal with people. He saw Mr. Campbell leave his house, carrying what appeared to be hunting gear, and walk toward his pickup truck. He would wait until Mr. Campbell drove away before going on.

Kevin was reaching over his seat for another paper when he heard the sound: a tearing high-pitched scream racing toward ultrasonic. A moment of unnatural silence followed, then a short final explosion. Something huge crashed through the roof of the Campbell house, raining down a shower of jagged debris.

A car parked across the street from the Campbell house exploded and burst into flames. Then something hit the hood of his car, splattering a bloody fluid over the windshield, and slowly slid over his hood, like a ruptured jellyfish, onto the ground.

His first thought was that Washington had been attacked, possibly by Russians, in a sneak attack like Pearl Harbor. It meant that he wouldn't have to deliver the rest of his papers. People were running out of their houses toward the burning car. Everyone seemed to be shouting. Someone said that it was an airplane crash. He quickly got out of his car thinking that he would make a run for it but then realized that he would be safer inside the car. He jumped back into the car and, grabbing his cell phone, and hurriedly dialed 911.

CHAPTER 2

February 10
Saturday, 8:00 a.m.

It was one of those Saturday mornings that Frank Adams preferred to stay in bed longer than usual. The thermometer outside his window was dead on freezing, and rain fell in gray waves, coating everything, including the thermometer, in a thick icy glaze. The phone rang. He rolled over, thinking he wouldn't answer. It would stop ringing after a while. It did. Then the phone rang once more. He threw the covers off him, wrapped a blanket over his shoulders, walked over to the thermostat, and slowly turned it up to a comfortable seventy degrees. The phone was still ringing. He picked up the handset and considered letting it drop back down.

"Uh, Mr. Adams? Is this Mr. Frank Adams?" The voice was female and had a note of desperation in it.

"Yes."

"I'm sorry to call you like this," she said. "I know it's Saturday morning—"

"I'm glad to know that you are aware of it," Frank said, trying to keep the irritation out of his voice.

"I want to employ you, Mr. Adams, and Monday morning might be too late. Can I meet you somewhere?"

"What sort of employment? And who are you?"

"I don't want to discuss it over the phone."

"Of course, but it might save us both some time and trouble if you know that I don't work as a security guard, and I definitely don't do surveillance work."

"I'm aware of your specialties, Mr. Adams. Where can we meet?"

"My office, in about two hours?"

"Fine."

The phone went dead on the other end, and Frank Adams, Accident Investigative Consultant, carefully lowered the phone's handset back into its cradle. Getting consulting work in his specialty had not always been this easy, especially when he first started out in this business. He did a few surveillance jobs back then to pay the rent for his office and apartment. His early retirement from the National Transportation Safety Board (NTSB) was just enough to keep him going.

He had enjoyed his work at NTSB and really did not want to retire at fifty-five years of age. He had put in thirty good years and was convinced that his work had saved lives.

NTSB was not, strictly speaking, a regulatory agency. Nevertheless, the principal responsibility of NTSB was to determine the probable cause of an aircraft accident and make regulatory recommendations to the FAA based on their findings. Industries subject to regulation learned many decades ago that they could alter the course of regulation through influence and pressure. Elected officials always needed money and friends. Industry officials often courted or befriended government employees who were sympathetic to industry.

Regulated industry also realized that it was much more efficient, less visible to the public, and cheaper to prevent or change proposed regulation before it got to the regulatory agency.

Frank had tolerated this "regulator capture" for years. However, on the last accident he worked on, his safety recommendations were again declined as not beneficial to public safety and cost prohibitive to the airline.

That was it for Frank. He put in for early retirement and as soon as the paperwork cleared and he had obtained the proper licensing, he opened an office as a private accident investigator.

Accident investigation work did not come easily, and the bills had to be paid so, he found work as a security guard for a couple of weeks in a department store until he saw an elderly woman of faded grandeur clumsily shoplifting lacy underwear. He went immediately to the staff locker room, tore off his oversized "rent a cop" suit, got back into his comfortable corduroy jacket, and left.

After that he found other unpleasant jobs to make ends meet. However, in the last few months, his business had improved. In addition to the recently acquired mortgage on his District apartment building, he could now afford his small office on K Street NW, and a part-time secretary. He was still driving a ten-year-old Chevy, though.

When the seemingly polar air in his apartment gradually reached the temperature underneath his blanket, he emerged from his cocoon. He took a quick shower, slipped on his bath robe, and wiped the condensation off the medicine cabinet mirror. Since his two-day stubble was wet and soft from the shower, he decided not to use shaving cream. He had never liked the messy, troublesome soap from the beginning of his adolescence. He took out his razor and for a moment did something that he had not done in twenty years: he looked carefully at his face in the mirror. His dark hair was showing sprinkles of grey. His hazel eyes, though still clear, were accented by small crow's feet at the corners. His previously small nose looked slightly larger, and small, red veins were beginning to show in his cheeks. He remembered his doctor warning him about this if he continued to drink whiskey at his current rate.

After shaving he dressed, put on a tie and jacket along with polished dress shoes, and decided, if time permitted, he would grab breakfast in the lobby coffee shop of his office building before meeting his prospective client.

There wasn't time. The battery in his Chevrolet had died peacefully during the night. After calling for a tow, he skipped and slipped on untreated patches of ice to the nearest subway station. The train was fifteen minutes late and smelled of overheated electrical equipment when it arrived. The car was empty except for a few stone-faced passengers who were unhappily on their way to Saturday jobs.

Walking the three blocks to his office was a glacial nightmare. Despite the occasional scatterings of sand and salt crystals, each step had to be carefully planned. Everything and everyone seemed to be moving at half speed, except for the motorized traffic roaring along as usual, heedless of the slick, black ice, dodging other vehicles and pedestrians with reckless agility.

A woman was waiting outside his office door. She was tall, in her early forties, and tastefully dressed. Frank detected the aroma of old money in her understated elegance.

"Mr. Adams?"

"Yes."

The woman smiled hesitantly. Frank inserted his key card. Metal clicked and buzzers buzzed. He opened the door and motioned for her to go in.

The office was as cold as his apartment. His office was a rather simple affair.It had a carpeted reception area, a small conference room, and an even smaller private office. The expensive mahogany and leather furniture belied his tight budget. He'd picked it all up second hand from an attorney who was selling out before going to "Club Fed" for embezzlement. He turned up the thermostat, took off his coat and sat behind his desk, waving her to a chair in front of him. She drew her camel hair coat tighter around her neck and body.

"It should warm up quickly," Frank said weakly. "What can I do for you, Miss . . .?"

"Before I tell you my name, I want to explain the situation. I'm speaking to you in total confidence, Mr. Adams."

"Of course," Frank said.

She paused, searching his face with her eyes, then resumed dispassionately as someone describing a familiar story. "You remember that airplane accident in Oxon Hill about a month ago?"

"Yes, I think there were three fatalities in that accident?"

"Yes. My husband Charles; Mark Asbury, another executive for the company; and the pilot, of course."

"I am very sorry to hear it." Frank said. She looked tearful for a moment, and her bottom lip quivered slightly. Then she said, "Yes, My husband. . ."

Frank waited for the woman to regain her composure.

"Yes. They were headed somewhere. Charles said it was for business, but he didn't say where they were going or what the business was. It was the first time he did that," she said, looking down at her hands. "He always told me everything."

"It was a company plane?" Frank asked.

"Yes." She said. "Charles was very proud of it."

"So, what would you like me to do for you?" Frank asked carefully.

"I want you to investigate the accident."

"Wouldn't you rather wait for the determination of the National Transportation Safety Board before taking this step?"

"They won't find anything. There wasn't much left of the plane or anyone on board."

"You would be amazed at what the NTSB can do," Frank said. "But what do you think I can do?"

"My lawyer said you're one of the best in your field and that you sometimes work as a consultant for the Safety Board in this type of case."

"They haven't called me on this one."

"That's what I mean. It probably looks like just another general aviation accident to them, but I don't think that it was. I believe my husband was murdered. I want you to—"

"Why do you suspect that?" Frank interjected.

"Mostly intuition based on how he was acting before he left . . . that sort of thing." She looked down at her hands again, wringing them in her lap.

Frank's second impression of her was that she was educated, wealthy, and able to control her emotions. *This is no neurotic nutjob widow,* he thought.

"Just how was he acting?" Frank asked.

"Tense, nervous. He would leave, sometimes suddenly, and wouldn't return for hours. In one sense, it was the way he usually acted when there was something important on his mind. But this was different." She fidgeted with her small handbag. "You know," she said, looking up at Frank, "I think I will have a cup of coffee, if you don't mind."

"Sure," Frank said. He got up from his desk and walked over to a small rectangular table where a large metal coffee pot was set up and ready to serve. He poured a large cup of coffee into a mug. "Cream and sugar?" he asked.

She shook her head. "Just black, please."

Frank handed her the cup of steaming hot coffee. She slowly took a couple of sips and closed her eyes. "God! That's good!" she said. "Anyway, before my husband's death, he seemed secretive and edgy. There were several phone calls that he took behind closed doors, but I could hear the strain in his voice. And when I asked him about it, he just ignored me."

"How would you characterize your marriage? Mrs. . . . ?"

The woman shrugged. "I might as well tell you. My name is Helen Rawlson and my husband is, or was, Charles Rawlson. He was CEO at Amertex electronics. The company designs, tests and manufactures electronic flight instruments—something they call integrated guidance systems and avionics—that sort of thing. It's highly competitive and cutting-edge stuff as they say."

"It's my father's company, and—" Her voice grew stronger. "If you're trying to ask me if my husband was having an affair, the answer is no." There was a twinge of alarm in her voice. "Oh, he did have an occasional flirtation, but it never amounted to anything. Men like my husband often have women throwing themselves at them. But he was loyal, considerate, and wouldn't deliberately do anything to hurt anyone. I know my husband," she firmly asserted—*or was it indignantly*, Frank wondered.

"My specialty is aircraft accident investigation, not murder, Mrs. Rawlson."

"I only want you to find the evidence, Mr. Adams. I know it's there."

"Have you spoken with anyone at the Safety Board about this?" Frank asked.

"Oh, yes. They're all very nice and polite, but they don't tell me anything."

"What about the police?"

"They were at the scene, of course, but they're letting the Board handle the investigation."

"Do you know if your husband was having trouble at work? Did he have any enemies, any debts?"

"He probably had some enemies, but mostly of the jealous kind, nobody that he really hurt. We also had no major debts. Our home is paid for and so are our vehicles. Charles scrupulously avoided debt."

Frank leaned forward on his elbows. His brow furrowed as he searched her eyes, looking for what she was not telling him.

"I'll pay anything you ask," she said. "I've tried elsewhere, but you're the only person really qualified for this. I wouldn't ask you to do anything dangerous or illegal, Mr. Adams."

Frank wasn't sure why he reached into his desk drawer and pulled out a contract. It was, after all, his line of work, and while he preferred working for companies or corporations, he didn't have a rule against working for individuals. Mrs. Rawlson had a legitimate interest. Perhaps it was her obvious refinement, poise, intelligence, and the most beautiful dark blue eyes he had ever seen.

He handed her the papers, and she read them without changing her expression. She seemed accustomed to reading legal documents.

"This sounds straightforward enough, Mr. Adams, and I'm encouraged by your businesslike approach."

She signed the papers, then wrote out a check. "Your retainer," she said, proffering the deposit. "Is there anything else I can tell you?" she asked.

"Yes. You could make a list of your husband's friends and people he had conflicts with in the past, what his interests were, what his financial and career concerns were—that type of thing. Anything you can remember about them."

"I could write a book, Mr. Adams."

"Please don't. Just the important facts of his life, that's all."

"When would you like it?"

"By Tuesday at the latest."

She sighed. "I'll try."

"Will you be in the area for the next few days, Mrs. Rawlson?"

"Yes, at home. I may have guests for the weekend."

Frank slid a small memo pad across his desk in front of Mrs. Rawlson. "Would you leave a number where you can be reached most of the time?"

She jotted her phone number on the memo pad and handed it to him. "Is that all for now?" she asked. She seemed more confident, more like the lady of the house speaking to one of her servants.

"Yes," Frank said, "I'll call if there is a problem. If you have any further questions, you have my phone number."

She smiled cordially. Frank returned it and offered his hand as they rose from their chairs.

"I won't hesitate. Thank you again," she said.

She moved gracefully like a runway model, as if she were always conscious of the striking parts of her figure. The camel hair coat, now draped casually over her shoulders, enhanced them.

After she left, he took out a microcassette recorder from his desk drawer and turned it on.

"Vickie, start a client file on a Mrs. Charles Rawlson. Date: February tenth, 1996, retained to investigate aircraft accident in which husband died. Suspects foul play. Find out what you can about her . . . you know, the standard form."

He switched off the recorder and put it back into the drawer, then carefully put Mrs. Rawlson's check into his shirt pocket.

The coffee shop was open, and Frank sat at his favorite table in the corner so he could see the doorway, a habit he had developed in the Army. Despite this, he was surprised by a voice nearby.

"What happened? Forget what day it was?"

Joan Kalen had been a waitress at the coffee shop for three years since Frank's first visit to the place. She was somewhere in her sixties, her face betraying evidence of a botched face lift, with blonde hair that reached her shoulders. Her clear, gray eyes, however, were still bright and cheerful. She had an acting background in local theater and a little television work, so she enjoyed a little notoriety with her favorite customers.

"Darling," Frank said, giving as good as he got, "I want you to get some new material. Then get yourself a new uniform and a new hairdo so that when I force myself out of bed, trudge through icy streets in the biting, cold wind just to come to this elite coffee shop, I might not recognize you."

"You're such a sweetheart, Frank. I would ask how your love life is, but I think I already know. Condolences." She smiled.

"I'll have what passes for coffee here and one of those brick doughnuts."

She returned after a few minutes with Frank's coffee and doughnut.

"Joan, do you know anything about a guy named Charles Rawlson?" Frank asked.

She placed his breakfast in the center of the table, along with a glass of water, splashing some onto the table. "Sorry, love. It's a big town, you know. Ask me about the Kennedys, the Carters, or the Alexanders, and I can help you. But the Rawlsons? Sorry, no can do."

"Who are the Alexanders?" Frank asked.

"Long story, sweetheart. Enjoy your breakfast. I've got work to do!"

For the time being, it wasn't necessary to know about Mr. Rawlson. That would come later after he had seen the wreckage and talked with Joe Hunter. He finished the doughnut and coffee and left the money for Joan on the table along with the usual 20 percent tip.

When he got back to his office, Frank called the auto repair garage where he had most of the repair work done on his car. They always took his checks without a flicker of hesitation. They would put a battery in his car and have it ready by noon.

He leafed through his office phone book for Joe Hunter's home number, dialed it, and waited.

"What?" Joe's voice was thick with sleep and irritation. Joe had been a colleague at the National Transportation Safety Board and his assistant on many investigations.

"Won't you be late for work, Joe?" teased Frank.

"What the hell? It's Saturday morning! Have you looked outside?"

"I'm awfully sorry, Joe. I thought it was Monday. Really sorry."

There was a long, heavy silence. Then Frank could hear muttering in the background.

"Jesst . . . ammuutit . . . sheeeat . . . tell him to . . . grrr . . . ssst . . . okay, Frank. What do you need?"

"Thanks, Joe. I appreciate it."

"You always do, Frank. What is it?"

"A client wants me to investigate an accident that happened about a month ago in the Oxon Hill area."

"Yeah, I know it. I'm working on it."

"Where is the wreckage being held?"

"In a hangar next to Potomac Airfield. You know it?"

"I think so. Who's running the operation?"

"A retired airline pilot named Alfred De Marco, operating out of a Quonset hut nearby."

"Joe, I want to see the wreckage. How about calling De Marco for me?"

"Why?" Joe asked.

"I told you; I'm working on a private case."

"Yeah, but for what? What are you interested in?"

"The woman thinks her husband might have been murdered."

"Frank, we've gone over the wreckage. It's clean."

"And the probable cause?"

"You know I can't discuss that with you now."

"I just want a look, Joe. That's all."

There was another long silence. Joe sighed, then said, "All right, when do you want to see it?"

Frank glanced at his watch. "It'll take about half an hour to get there. I have to get my car fixed . . . say around noon?"

"Anything else, friend?"

"Not at the moment. Are you going to be home tonight in case I want to stop by to share some of that twenty-five-year-old single malt?"

"You're so polite, Frank. And really, very thoughtful and considerate. I simply can't understand why you never remarried."

"I may have a calling for the priesthood. Don't want to mess that up."

Explosive laughter on the other end for a few moments. "All right," Joe snorted, "I'll see you later, Reverend."

Frank hung up and quickly jotted down De Marco's name and number. A wave of hunger gurgled in his stomach. He hurriedly locked his office and took the elevator to the ground floor for a proper breakfast.

CHAPTER 3

F rank only made one wrong turn on the way to the airfield, but it cost him a quarter of an hour driving around in a curvaceous maze of high-priced houses, drawing uncomfortable glances from snow shovelers and dog walkers. After many wild guess turns, he blundered back on to the correct road and followed the signs to Potomac Airfield.

Alfred De Marco had the look of a man who was used to making life and death decisions. His eyes met Frank's straight on and seemed to lock onto them like some inescapable beam. Frank sensed that the man could be either a loyal and unselfish friend or a ruthless and determined enemy. There seemed to be no in-between with Mr. De Marco. Not wasting time on social amenities or gray areas of conversation, he invited Frank into his office and showed him a chair. To his surprise, the other chair was occupied by a lanky teenager engrossed in a Marvel comic book.

"My grandson," De Marco gestured. "He likes to hang around on the weekends. Thinks I'm going to let him become a pilot," De Marco growled. The boy smiled and introduced himself as Tony, then went back to reading his comic.

The office walls were covered in pictures and keepsakes of his career: awards for air combat service in Vietnam, trophies, and models of various types of transport aircraft he had flown.

"Nice little operation you've got here," Frank said.

"Thank you. It was a mess when I took it over ten years ago. So, you want to see the wreckage?" De Marco asked.

"Joe said to let you see anything you wanted, but I'm afraid there isn't much. People are still bringing in pieces of that plane. Just a couple of days ago a fella came in here with a section from the wing flap."

Tony looked up. "Said he found it on top of his garage where it had punched a small hole in the roof!"

"Don't see how it could have done that," De Marco countered. "The thing was as light as a feather. But that's for him and the insurance company to fight about. No tellin' how much more is lying around on people's houses or in the tops of trees. If this snow and freezing rain keep up, it'll be a while until it all gets washed down."

"I can believe it," Frank said.

De Marco looked at his grandson, "You know, I haven't turned a wheel in a week. We shoulda gone to Florida like your grand mom wanted. Right, kid?" he said to the boy. "But what the hell." De Marco shrugged. "Come on. I'll walk over there with you."

They half walked and half slid across the deserted, icy runway and tie-down area to the hangar where the remains of the jet were being kept. Clear, jewel-like stalactites of ice hung from the cluster of small planes that were tied down in the aircraft parking area. The ground crunched under their feet, and ice-coated grass tinkled as their thick, glossy coverings shattered.

The hangar was a rusty, metal structure that looked like a large barn. There were a few airplanes in various states of repair toward the rear of the building. A heavy wire mesh wall separated the room at the back of the hangar. The room was used to store machine parts and runway maintenance equipment. The wreckage was laid out on the large floor of the hangar. Twisted and mangled fragments of the jet's components were carefully placed in their customary positions had the plane been undamaged.

"One thing about airplane accidents like this that never fails to strike me is how thousands of pounds of machinery can be reduced to a handful of metal bits," De Marco said.

"Yes, I know. You would think there would have to be more to it than that." Frank walked over to the left wing and crouched next to it on one heel.

The wing showed considerable buckling and twisting, especially near the tip section. He picked up a small piece of the outboard section and examined it.

"The spar, rib, and skin all show considerable signs of g-force overloading. The right and left stabilizers are in the same condition," Frank said. "It certainly looks like it came apart in the air."

"That's probably what will go in the NTSB's report," said De Marco.

"But it could've been a hundred reasons." He continued. "The way this looks, I don't think we'll ever fully know."

Frank walked over to the remains of the fuselage. "Any sign of tampering or a fire on board; any evidence of a bomb?"

"Again, with total destruction like this, it's hard to say. There are indications of torsion and compression overloads." De Marco picked up a part of the twisted aircraft and examined it like a geologist looking over a strangely shaped rock.

"It's very unusual for this type of aircraft to come apart like this," Frank said, "I don't think I've ever seen one like this before. The pilot must have been doing some crazy things with the controls. This is what you see when aerodynamic forces overload an airplane. Things twist and bend until they finally break." He looked around at the debris. "The other damage was caused when the biggest part of the airplane hit the ground and burned."

The wreckage still bore the strong odor of JP-4 fuel. The cockpit looked like it should after hitting the ground from a straight fall of several thousand feet. None of the aircraft's components had any signatures of an internal explosion.

"It looks to me like the pilot just lost it in the clouds," De Marco said. "It went into a graveyard spiral, got overstressed somehow, and came apart just before it hit the ground. No doubt the pilot was yanking and pulling on the yoke all the way to the ground."

Frank remembered his early training in spatial disorientation. Spatial disorientation usually happened when one entered instrument flight conditions. The instruments told you that you were going straight and level, but every sense in your mind and body told you that you were turning. It sometimes took every bit of mental strength to believe your instruments rather than trusting your brain.

"It's that instinct for self-preservation that keeps you fighting even though you know what you're doing is only making it worse," Frank said.

"Why do you suppose he didn't use his secondary flight instruments. They're not powered by the same system that powers the primary flight instruments." De Marco said.

"You know how it is, Al. You're a professional pilot," Frank said. "At first there is denial: 'This can't be happening to me.' That takes a few valuable seconds. Next comes fear or panic—a few more valuable seconds. Then fighting through the fear and panic to try to figure things out. He was probably doing the wrong thing the entire time. When he broke out of the clouds and saw the ground coming at him, he overstressed the controls, and the airplane came apart. His speed had to be off the clock."

De Marco shook his head slowly, as if processing what had probably happened.

Something happened in that cockpit that was beyond the pilot's experience, Frank thought. Frank envisioned the pilot struggling to get ahead of what was occurring to the airplane, and knowing he was running out of time. He imagined the pilot fighting at the controls and screaming against the inevitable outcome.

"I don't think this would have happened if there had been a second pilot," De Marco said.

"Maybe not, but I doubt we'll ever know."

Suddenly, both men were startled by the loud bang of the hangar door opening and closing. They turned to see Joe Hunter walking toward them.

"I just couldn't get back to sleep knowing you were poking around here. What have you found so far?" Joe asked.

"Nothing that isn't obvious," Frank said.

"Yeah, it looks cut and dried, doesn't it? It just keeps bugging me how a highly experienced pilot can lose it like that even though I know it does happen," Joe said. "The same thing happened last November in California with another very experienced pilot. Augured in after coming out of the clouds inverted. Witnesses said they saw the plane start to roll out, but there wasn't enough altitude. There was too much cloud cover for anyone to get a good look. It happens more times than I like to think."

De Marco nodded.

"I don't suppose this bird had an in-flight recorder?" Frank asked.

Joe shook his head. "I've tried to have 'em installed on these biz jets, but the corporate interests against it are too strong. You know how it is; all they have to do is pick up the phone and call the congressman they support. Then the congressman gets word to the Secretary of Transportation who then tells the FAA what to do and say. Frank, you worked for NTSB. I've seen you lose it a few times when the Board's decision was obviously influenced. Big money will always find a way. You know that don't you, Frank?"

Frank nodded slightly. "I know," he said and paused. Then Frank pulled Joe out of earshot. "What did the guy in the tower have to say?"

Joe shrugged. "According to him and the tower recording, it seemed like a normal flight, the usual assortment of mix-ups, repeats, and clarifications. Just before it started to go wrong, the controller noticed a sudden loss of altitude, then a gradual turn to the left. He asked 'em for a confirmation of heading and altitude, and the pilot asked him to standby. The controller said there was nothing in the tone of the pilot's voice to indicate a critical problem. Then the transponder went out intermittently, and the next radar sweep showed the plane down to six thousand feet. The next sweep was down to twenty-five hundred, and nothing was there on the next sweep."

"There was no transmission from the pilot during this time?" Frank asked.

"Not a word."

"Where are the instruments?"

"We sent what we could find to the manufacturer for analysis."

"I take it you haven't heard from them."

"Not yet, but we expect to hear from them soon."

"Who did the medical work?"

"Dr. Edward Mandan, the local medical examiner at Good Samaritan Hospital. His report came in last week."

"Can I see it?"

"Sure, but you'll have to wait until Monday." Joe sighed. "I can't keep that stuff on me . . . you know that. Hell, the world can't hump seven days a week because you have a client," he said as though he were confronting an impatient subordinate.

"I know, Joe. Don't get all bent out of shape. I used to work for the government too. How about taking me over to the site?"

Joe glanced at his watch. "I'll take you over there, but I won't be able to stay."

"Okay I'll follow you," Frank said.

They gave De Marco a departing handshake and walked back across the airfield. The wind had shifted to the north and started to blast cold shock waves of freezing air over the runway. The rain had changed to hard grains of snow.

"Looks like it's going to clear up," Frank said to Hunter.

"Yeah, but it won't do me any good. Everything'll be frozen rock hard by tomorrow."

Frank tried his best to keep his old Chevy close to Joe's Porsche RS911. It wasn't easy following the RS911 through the high-speed traffic of the beltway or the twisting suburban streets of Oxon Hill. They approached a cluster of modest homes, most apparently built from the same floor plan, and stopped next to an empty lot that had been trampled by heavy moving equipment. Except for a few shattered walls and parts of the charred foundation, nothing remained of the home.

"This is where the main part of the fuselage came down," Joe explained. "Right dead center of this guy's house. He was a lucky SOB. He had just left the house to do some fishing or something like that when the impact of the Citation blew his house away. Fortunately, there was no one inside—he apparently lives alone, and I can see why. Just between you and me, he strikes me as a real piece of work. The rest of the debris extends in a southeasterly and northwesterly direction, but most of the parts were found on the southeast axis. The largest portion, the left wing, landed in the street over there and set a car on fire. The right wing landed in the shrubbery over there."

Joe pointed to a distant line of trees to the west. "The wreckage was scattered all around and, from the debris pattern, the stuff must have floated out of the sky like confetti. Look around if you want, but I should warn you that the people here are getting pretty tired of official types stomping around in their backyards."

Joe got back into his car and drove off. Frank walked over to the disturbed ground. It had been thoroughly gone over. Nothing remained but bits of construction material with brown, chewed-up earth and puddles of freezing slush. He looked up at the clearing sky. Broken gray stratus clouds with ragged silver edges raced to the southeast. Behind this jigsaw puzzle of clouds, the sky was clear blue. Somewhere up there, a very beautiful airplane had come apart despite all the safety precautions built into it and killed three people in a very hideous way.

"You won't find nothing here."

The voice came from behind him. Frank turned to see a large man in his fifties, dressed in heavy outdoor clothes and army boots, walking toward him.

"They've been all over here like a swarm of ants. Name's Irwin Campbell," he said, introducing himself. "That was my place." Campbell nodded in the direction of the remains of a modest house several hundred feet away.

"Frank Adams. I'm an investigative consultant."

"That so. Sort of a private detective, huh?"

"Sort of."

"I'm glad I caught you. I've been staying with my sister down the street. Me and my buddies are going on the hunting trip we missed out on a month ago because of that." He nodded toward the wreckage. "Only now, we can only go bow hunting, it being February. You workin' for the company, I suppose?"

"What company?"

"The one that owned the airplane."

"No, I'm looking into the accident on behalf of a victim."

"Some kind of suit or insurance deal, huh?"

"Something like that."

"Yeah, it figures. Somebody's always trying to sue somebody for somethin'. My turn'll come soon," he said, absently rubbing his hands together, cupping them and blowing into them.

"Did you see the accident, Mr. Campbell?"

"I sure as hell did. I never seen anything like it the whole time I was in the service. Like I said, me and a few buddies were going hunting. They had come by to pick me up, and on the way out to the van I heard this plane, like right above me." Campbell pointed to the sky. "It was getting louder and louder, like it was coming straight at me. It seemed like the whole inside of a cloud had suddenly lit up. Then something that looked like a small submarine with tiny wings popped out of the clouds and was falling straight for me. I tell you, I just couldn't move." Remembered terror filled his eyes. "I just kept watching that thing come at me. Then I seen streaks of fire bust out of the clouds behind it." Campbell simulated an explosion with his hands. "That did it. I ran like hell for cover and dove under that truck over there." He pointed to a late model pickup truck that was parked in a driveway about a hundred yards away. "I heard it hit the ground. Sounded like a box full of empty cans hitting all at once. Stuff was raining down all over the place. I was just hoping and praying that nothin' hit the truck I was hiding under.

Then, all of a sudden, there was an explosion. My neighbor's car across the street from my house was in flames, and their roof was caved in. I don't know . . . it seems terrible now, but I had to laugh. I looked over at my buddies, and they was all crouched down inside the van. Then the doors flew open and all three of 'em started running like mad down the street until I lost sight of 'em. I laughed till I cried. I know I shouldn't have, but I couldn't help it.

"When things quieted down and stuff stopped falling, we all ran for what was left of my house to see what we could do, but there was nothing nobody could do. There just wasn't nothing left. I seen the top of a man's head in the debris. So, I pulled a piece of sheet metal out of the way thinking I could get to him, but that was all there was, just the top of a man's head. I tell you, Mr. Adams, I'm a grown man and I seen a lot in Vietnam, but I had to turn away from that and near vomit. Even now, I just can't seem to forget about it. Everybody's getting tired of me talking about it, but I can't seem to stop. My house is gone and everything in it. It's like my whole life, past and present, has been wiped out. Insurance man came out and I'm gettin' some money, but he can't give me back my past. Who can I see about that, huh? Who's going to make it right?"

Frank shook his head slowly in sympathy with the man. "Well, I'm very glad you told me, Mr. Campbell. And don't worry, you'll come out of this in time."

"Yeah, that's what everybody keeps telling me. I sure hope so. I'm about to go crazy thinking about it."

"One more thing," said Frank. "Did you hear any unusual noise coming from the engines before you saw the plane?"

"No, can't say I did. That's something I don't pay much attention to. You know, airplanes are always flying over here. You get to where you sort of block out the noise after a while. But when I got to thinking about it, the engines sounded like they were screaming louder than usual, but I can't say for sure."

"Well, I'm afraid you're right, Mr. Campbell, there doesn't seem to be anything here."

Finding something was always a long shot after this much time had passed. Even so, the Board might have missed something, but that was not likely. It appeared to Frank that this might be a dead end. He would have to focus on the Rawlsons' friends and colleagues.

"Nevertheless, Mr. Campbell, if you think of anything, give me a call," Frank said.

He pulled a business card from his coat pocket and handed it to Campbell. Campbell looked at the card, turned it over several times as though he expected to see something on the back, then slipped it into his shirt pocket.

"My home phone number is on there also, so don't hesitate if you remember something."

"Sure thing," Campbell said. "You sure you're not working with the government?"

"No, as I said, I'm a private consultant."

"That's too bad cause somebody's going to pay for this, and it ought to be the government."

The man looked strangely deflated, and without another word, he turned and walked away with his hands stuffed into his pants pockets just as his hunting friends were driving up.

CHAPTER 4

February 10
Saturday, 4:00 p.m.

Joe was leaning over a layout of aircraft accident photographs in his living room when he looked up to see Frank standing at the door smiling and holding a bottle of twenty-five-year-old single malt Scotch whiskey.

Joe got up and answered the door. "Come in, come in," he said, relieved to be taken away from the pictures for a while.

"Homework?"

"You know the drill, Frank. This work is never done, and we're always trying to play catch-up."

"My case?" Frank asked as he sat down on the couch.

"No, this is something new. A lumberjack in Oregon was showing the boys what he could do with a Citabria."

Frank looked through the pictures of the mangled remains of the Citabria. Very little was immediately identifiable. "He showed 'em all right," he said. "You know, Joe, this is a really ghastly business you're in."

"Ha! You should talk. The snooping around you do, it's a wonder you haven't been arrested on a Peeping Tom charge."

"So, what's that in your hand?" Joe asked.

"I never break a promise, Joe. You ought to know that by now."

With great fanfare, Frank opened the bottle of Glenlivet and slowly poured the whiskey into two tumblers. "So, what do you want or need?" Joe asked.

"I want to see the medical examiner's reports, and I want to know your opinion on the probable cause," Frank said.

"I told you what I could earlier, but I'll tell you this. There wasn't enough left of the bodies to do an autopsy. We simply picked up all the body parts we could find and sent them out for DNA and toxicology analysis." Joe smiled and glanced away. "Why don't you wait until the blue cover comes out?"

"I haven't got until next year, and your hypotheticals won't cut it."

Joe walked over to his desk. He reached into a stack of folders, pulled out a thin one and dropped it on Frank's lap. "I wish I could make you angry, Frank."

Frank laughed. "Not me, Joe. I've been gifted by nature with a subsurface alligator hide."

"I know, I know. These are the lab reports. It also contains the toxicology results."

Frank leafed through the report. "Huh . . . trace amounts of alcohol in the passengers, which must have been consumed very early in the morning? What a way to stop a hangover."

"That's not funny, Frank."

"Sorry. The pilot was clean, though."

"Yes, he was. No evidence of impairment of any kind. But there is something interesting. Come by the office on Monday."

It was about six in the evening when Frank arrived back home and climbed the long flight of stairs to his apartment on the top floor. He waited on the top stair for a moment to catch his breath and vowed, once again, to install a small two-occupant lift as soon as finances allowed. He went straight to the small bar that he kept in one corner of the book cabinet behind his desk and emptied the remains of a bottle of scotch into a highball glass, poured in a dollop of soda, and picked up the phone to call Mrs. Rawlson.

"Rawlson residence. Good evening."

"May I speak with Mrs. Rawlson, please?"

"Whom shall I say is calling?"

"Frank Adams."

"Thank you. One moment."

Soon Mrs. Rawlson was on the line. Her voice sounded weak and shaky as though she was recovering from an illness.

"Mrs. Rawlson, do you think there is a chance I could stop by and see your father?"

"When would you like to see him?"

"Would tomorrow be convenient?"

"I suggest you call first. He's a very private man, and he's still in shock over the death of Charlie. Do you need his address and number?"

"Yes, I do," Frank said as he proceeded to jot down the information she provided. Mrs. Rawlson's father was Richard Russell, the president and owner of Amertex.

After a brief pause she asked. "Anything else? Any. . . uh, developments? How is it going so far?"

"I'll let you know as soon as I have something to report," Frank replied. "Probably in the next couple of days. Thanks again."

"Ah, yes," she said, unable to keep the disappointment out of her voice at the sudden termination of the conversation. "Later then," she said and hung up.

Frank took a long drink of his scotch and called Richard

Russell. A man answered and, in a formal tone of voice, informed him that Mr. Russell was not seeing anyone for the remainder of the weekend.

"Please explain to him that I'm investigating the death of his son-in-law on behalf of his daughter, Mrs. Rawlson, and it's important that I see him."

"Ah, I see. May I have your name and number, sir? And I'll have Mr. Russell get in touch with you at his earliest convenience."

It was late when Frank pushed his shoes off and propped his feet up on the nearest footstool. He needed to digest everything that Hunter and De Marco had said. He flipped on the sound system—that was how he had to refer to it since adding a new CD player. He still had his old Pioneer turntable and stereo and several stacks of LPs. He could never bring himself to get rid of them, and now it seemed LPs were enjoying a renaissance.

He pushed in his favorite CD, walked back to his comfortable chair, propped his feet back up on the footstool, reopened the bottle of Glenlivet that he had rescued from Joe's house, and lost himself in the lovely voice of Irene Kral singing delightfully, but mournfully, of love and loss.

CHAPTER 5

February 11
Sunday, 8:00 a.m.

The phone woke him early the next morning. Frank sat up, startled, feeling the stress in his lower back and neck, and slowly surveyed the room. An empty glass lay on the floor next to a dark liquid stain in the rug. The CD player had switched itself off, but the red light on the amplifier still glowed. He fumbled for the phone.

"Mr. Adams? This is Richard Russell," a heavy male voice said on the other end. "What did you want to talk to me about?"

Mr. Russell was a man who got straight to the point.

"I'm investigating the accident that took the life of your son-in-law, Charles Rawlson, and I want to ask you some questions," Frank said, trying to sound awake and alert.

"I thought the feds were handling the investigation."

"They are. I'm working on behalf of Mrs. Rawlson."

"Helen? In what way?" Mr. Russell demanded.

"She wants me to make sure that it was an accident."

"Isn't that up to the feds?" Mr. Russell snapped. "Aren't they supposed to do that?"

Frank said, "I'll be direct, Mr. Russell. The National Transportation Safety Board's role is to determine the probable cause of the accident, and if they find evidence of a crime, the Board will report it to the police. The police handle any criminal investigation. The problem with accidents of this type is that there usually isn't enough left of the aircraft or the people in it to clearly establish criminality."

"So, you're a private investigator, like a private detective?"

"You could say that, but my specialty is accident investigation, which includes auto and aircraft. My primary focus, however, is aircraft accidents. I used to work directly for the NTSB and still do contract work for them on occasion."

"I see. Helen didn't mention any of this to me. It's very strange. Oh well, come over on Monday. I'll be here between one and five. The place is on Mill Road, about two miles off the main highway. The name is on the fence. We'll expect you."

After Mr. Russell hung up, Frank rechecked the scribbled list of things he needed to do he had made the night before, but he couldn't do anything of value until Monday. The whole country shuts down for the weekend. If anyone wanted to commit a murder and get away with it, Saturday morning was the best time, and surprise attacks were for Sunday.

February 12
Monday, 1:00 pm

The Russell estate was located several miles from the town of Middleburg, Virginia, in Louden County. Louden County was horse country, and it wasn't unusual to see fox hunters galloping through the fields and jumping over bushes and hedgerows with hunting horns blaring and dogs barking. For those who didn't care for hunting or horses, there was always the Country Club.

Middleburg had the appearance of a small, clean, rural town that a group of very rich people bought because they wanted a small, typical main-street, Rockwellian, American town lined with expensive clothing stores, chic coffee shops, art galleries, expensive restaurants, and book shops. It was relatively close to Dulles International Airport, which provided quick flights to Europe or California, and it was within easy commuting distance of Washington, DC. The average cost of a home was roughly $700,000, with estates like the Russell's selling for somewhere between $10 and $30 million. There is no place for poverty or poor people in Louden County, Virginia.

Finding the Russell estate wasn't as easy as it had sounded on the phone. After several stops to ask for directions, Frank made all the correct turns and found himself stopped in front of a tall iron gate flanked by CCTV cameras. He pressed the intercom, and a disembodied voice acknowledged him. An electronic whine rang out, a bolt clanked, and the gates swung open. He drove along the manicured gravel driveway lined on either side by a white post and rail fence and approached the circular courtyard in front of the house.

Built two hundred years ago in the Georgian style, the mansion stood on the highest part of a small but steep series of hills. Further down, along a small ridge, Frank saw a covered swimming pool, which was partially blocked from view by a procession of stately gray hardwood trees. Adjacent to the swimming pool was a sculpture garden dotted with life-sized marble and bronze figures glittering with icicles, and mature shrubberies blanketed in snow.

An elderly butler answered the door, murmured something unintelligible, and motioned for Frank to follow him. Frank did as he was bid and waited as the butler struggled to slide the heavy polished pocket doors of the library into their recesses. Mr. Russell was seated in a tall-backed leather chair and was gazing out a set of French windows taking in the expansive view of his formal garden and statuary. The butler approached and purred something to Mr. Russell, who remained motionless. The only word that Frank caught during this exchange was his own name.

"Anything to drink, Mr. Adams?" Mr. Russell asked before the butler left.

"No thanks," Frank replied, inching forward into the large, book-lined room.

Mr. Russell continued facing the window.

"Take a chair," he said, motioning toward a chair beside him.

Frank walked around a highly polished walnut partner desk in the center of the room and over to the chair indicated by Mr. Russell's barely visible hand.

Mr. Russell was in his mid-seventies; and his hair was still dark with just a few traces of gray. His eyes, set in dark circles, were as keen and clear as a young man's. He had regular features, spotted skin, and a smile that revealed unstained and perfectly aligned teeth. His face, however, was shaded and marked by lines of recent grief.

"If I seem to be a bit aloof, I'm sorry for it. It's just that Charlie's death remains a terrible shock. I never had a son until he married Helen. That's how we were, like father and son. I was even thinking about retiring. He was the only person I would have trusted with the business. Then this happened, and now you are suggesting that it might have been murder."

Mr. Russell leaned forward and poured brandy from a crystal decanter into a snifter, then offered it to Frank without a word. Frank shook his head slowly. Russell nodded slightly, sat back, and took a long sip. Frank couldn't help but notice a large portrait of an attractive woman in her mid-fifties hanging over the stone fireplace mantel. The picture had a small bouquet of roses on each side.

"My late wife," Mr. Russell said. "We met in college. She was majoring in education. Wanted to be a teacher, and she was for a while, then Helen came along, and after that we had a son, Gregory, but he died two days after his birth. The doctors tried to save him with surgery to correct a congenital intestinal disorder, but his body could not stand the stress and his condition couldn't be repaired. He died on the operating table. Poor little guy never opened his eyes, never saw his mother. My wife was killed last year in a car accident. The police said that she simply lost control of the car, crossed the median on Highway 50, and hit another car head-on. Both she and the other driver died at the scene. And now Charles. You see, Mr. Adams, tragedy does rain on the rich and poor alike," Mr. Russell said, his eyes welling up with tears.

"I am sorry, Mr. Russell," Frank said.

"No, no. I apologize for inflicting my troubles on you. I shouldn't have said anything." Mr. Russell waved his hand as if dismissing the subject.

After a brief hesitation, Frank said, "Your daughter simply wants her doubts cleared up. There hasn't really been any direct suggestion—"

"A doubt is a suggestion, Mr. Adams. And if there is anything to it—if someone did murder Charles—I want to know. I want the bastard brought to justice," Mr. Russell said, barely able to control the tremor in his voice.

Mr. Russell turned, his eyes meeting Frank's for a long moment. "You can count on my support all the way across the board," he said.

"Thank you, Mr. Russell." Frank felt pinned to his chair by Mr. Russell's intense gaze. "In that case, I do have a few questions. What was the nature of the business trip? Do you know where they were going?"

"Well, to answer that, I'd like to back up a bit. Amertek has been in negotiations with the US government for a very lucrative contract for quite some time. It's all very hush-hush. We were also approached in October by Dongan Manufacturing, a Chinese company that was interested in buying into Amertek. It was really quite a coup for Amertek, as Dongan is a well-known firm with a profitable track record. Charlie had trouble bringing Dongan to the table since they saw him as only a minor shareholder. He finally got Jerry Saunders, one of our VPs, to set up a meeting in Miami in November. All was going smoothly until I read in the paper that the deal was off. I didn't know anything about it! I was very upset with Charlie for keeping me out of the loop. So, he set up another meeting in January to see if he could save the situation. Saunders was supposed to go along on the trip with him to help grease the wheels, as they say, but he bailed at the last minute. That's why Mark Asbury was on board. Poor schmuck. He was just going as a witness and to take notes."

"So, this was the flight to Miami to meet Dongan again?"

"Yes."

"Did your son-in-law ever mention threats on his life?"

"Oh, the usual thing from disgruntled union members. I get them myself, mostly around contract time. Nothing ever comes of it. It's just a way of posturing and letting off steam, that's all."

"What about rivals or colleagues who might have envied his relationship with your family?"

"Oh yes, I'm sure he did have rivals. I try to encourage competition among my executives. It keeps them sharp and, on the ball, good for morale too."

"And maybe one of them felt that they didn't stand a chance as long as your son-in-law was around?" Frank suggested.

Mr. Russell raised his snifter of brandy to his lips. "That's a possibility, but this is not a new situation. I have been slowly retreating into retirement for quite some time. I had a heart attack about six months ago. I kept it as classified information from all the VPs. Charlie was the only one who knew about it. I know all my executives well. They are an ambitious bunch. And, as I said, I want them to be. So, my health was not something I wanted to fall into the mix of succession. But I don't think there is one of them who would ever seriously consider such a terrible alternative."

"I presume that you have a list of their names, addresses, and phone numbers?"

"Yes." Mr. Russell reached into his desk drawer and pulled out a folder. "This is a copy of the company directory. Every executive has one. It lists all our employees. The executives and officers are listed in the back." He flipped to a separate section on the last two pages of the directory. "To the left of the names is a letter code of each management position held in the company."

Frank took the pamphlet-size directory and thumbed through it briefly. "Thank you. May I keep this for a while?"

Mr. Russell hesitated. "I trust that you will be discreet. While the directory is not classified, it is closely held, and I want the privacy of my employees and executives respected as much as possible."

"Certainly," Frank said. He took a moment to look around the room. "Mr. Russell, this looks like more of an office than a library. Is this where you conduct your business?"

"For the most part, yes. I have an office at company headquarters in Leesburg as well, but this office is, shall I say, more private?"

"I understand completely."

"Now, is there anything else?"

"Actually, there is one other thing I want you to know. I'm not implying anything, only exploring all the possibilities. Was your daughter and son-in-law's marriage . . . stable? I mean, did Charles or your daughter mention any trouble between them?"

Mr. Russell lowered his glass. His eyes developed a cold blue flame. "That is one hell of an implication, Mr. Adams. I don't know if I like it at all."

"I didn't think you would, Mr. Russell, but people have been killed by their spouses before."

Mr. Russell smiled slightly. "That's true, but if any trouble of that kind existed, I didn't know about it. Furthermore, if there had been, Helen would have told me about it. You see, Mr. Adams, I have always had a very close relationship with my daughter."

Frank stood up. "Thank you for your time, Mr. Russell. If something comes up, can you be reached at your office this week?"

"No, I'll be in Anguilla for a couple of weeks."

"Can you be reached there?" Frank asked.

"No. I want complete privacy for a while. Helen is managing the business while I'm away, but if you really need to get in touch with me, you can call my secretary. He'll relay your communication to me."

Mr. Russell pressed a blue button on his desk. In a few moments, the old butler appeared in the doorway.

"Before you leave," Mr. Russell said, turning toward Frank, "do you have anything so far, other than my daughter's doubts, that would suggest foul play?"

"No, not a thing, sir."

"Good, good. I don't think I could take it after everything that's happened. Good day." Mr. Russell leaned back in his chair, snifter in hand, and resumed gazing at the bleak hillside with the frozen figures of his sculpture garden.

Frank followed the shuffling butler, resisting the urge to bound past him like an impatient Groucho Marx. The old man seemed to have no interest in the trivial, the unnecessary, and the wasteful intervals of life. *The daily journey to the door must be an arduous task for the old man,* Frank thought. *And his function in this house, where power resides and million-dollar deals are made, is, ironically, time saving.*

Back in his old Chevy Frank made a note on his mini cassette to have Vickie run a background check on all the executives, especially the higher-ups in the company, and to dig up what she could on the recent demise of Mrs. Russell.

CHAPTER 6

The drive to Alexandria normally took a little over forty minutes, but the day's weather increased the trip to an hour. Frank looked up at the soaring, glass face of the apartment complex that overlooked the Potomac. It matched the address given in the company's directory for Selma Green, the pilot's widow. He had to park several blocks away and walk against a tearing, frigid wind that lashed around buildings and picked up loose grit and trash, sending them stinging into his face and tinkling against the peripheral chain-link fence.

He explained to a bored security guard at the front desk that he wanted to see Selma Green, and he showed the guard his business card. The guard nodded and asked for more identification, so Frank showed him his driver's license, commercial pilot's certificate, investigator's license, and a credit card. The guard held up his hand, nodded, then said, "Okay, you can go up. Sign here." He pushed a blue cloth-bound book in front of him and pointed to a blank space. Frank scrawled his signature in the visitor's register. He glanced at other names in the register but didn't recognize any of them.

"Be sure to sign out when you leave. Don't forget the time," the guard warned. There was the threat of a possible firing squad in his tone.

The Greens' suite was located at the end of a short hallway. Frank pressed the bell once, and in a short moment, a woman of about thirty, her shoulder-length red hair done up in a twist, opened the door. She wore what the fashion magazines once called cocktail pajamas, and a highly embroidered satin gown. She stood in the doorway, one hand on her hip and the other holding the doorknob, and greeted him with, "Are you from the insurance company?" Her green eyes swept coldly over him.

"Not exactly."

She started to close the door, but Frank quickly held out one of his cards. She stopped just short of slamming the door on his wrist, made a sucking sound between her lips, and took the card.

She looked at it quickly, cast her eyes to one side, and said, "Christ, everybody in this town is a fucking consultant. Doesn't anyone have a real job?"

"I'm looking into the airplane accident that took your husband's life, Mrs. Green. And I was wondering whether you could help me," Frank said, trying not to sound intimidated.

"And you're not from the insurance company?" she asked, her thin eyebrows forming a horizontal question mark.

"No, sorry."

"You're sorry? I'm the one who's sorry. Christ! I don't know what's taking them so long. Goddamn insurance company!" She started to close the door again.

"They're probably waiting for the NTSB to complete their investigation," Frank interjected before the door closed.

The door stopped.

"You know something about that?"

"I used to work for the Board."

"That so? Well, come in then. It's a lousy day anyway. And I'm not doing anything but sitting around getting loaded."

She opened the door wider and waited for him to enter. As

she closed it behind him, Frank heard the click of an automatic lock engage.

"Don't worry, honey. I'm not going to hurt you," she said. "If my company gets too boring, you can just push this little yellow button on the doorknob—twist and presto. Want a drink?" she asked. "I've got a pitcher of martinis already made up."

"No, thank you," Frank said.

"Ah, come on. It's Monday. It's almost Saturday night and look outside."

Frank followed her into the living room and stopped to take in the view through a large window. A continuous stream of transport jets glided down into the confined and unforgiving airspace of Reagan National Airport. The gray Potomac carried slabs of ice resolutely downstream past the Woodrow Wilson Bridge and Mount Vernon to the salty waters of the Chesapeake Bay. The city itself seemed to glow orange in the last of the day's winter light. The ground below this tenth-floor apartment was already in shadow.

"I won't be long. I only want to ask you a few questions about your husband," Frank said.

He turned away from the view outside. The woman was sitting on the sofa with her legs stretched along its length, sipping a martini.

"How long had your husband been a pilot for Amertek Electronics?"

"You really are all business, aren't you? I must admit I find it rather charming in a man, and very unusual." She hesitated, then said, "Oh, he's been with Amertek for about three years."

"Did he ever get into any trouble? I mean, was he ever asked to do anything that he might have considered reprehensible or unethical?"

"Who, Tommy? Ha, that's a laugh. Tommy was as pure as

a ten-year-old virgin. If someone ever did proposition him, he would not have had sense enough to know it. Don't get me wrong. I mean, Tommy was a real nice boy, a saint, strictly the all-American type from Indiana, know what I mean?"

Frank flashed a slight smile. "Someone in his position is often privy to all kinds of information. Company people tend to speak and act freely on private jets. I thought he might have mentioned something to you or told you an anecdote in passing."

"No way. The only thing Tommy cared about was flying airplanes. A corrupt thought never entered his head."

She slid her legs to the floor and, carefully balancing her drink in her hand, stood up and walked toward Frank. She gently slipped her free hand over his shoulder.

"Now you . . . you're something else." She touched his forehead. "I'll bet that head is full of all sorts of deliciously evil thoughts and corruption."

"I think I'll have that drink now," Frank said. It seemed the politest way to get her to remove her hand from his shoulder and change the course of the conversation.

She took out a martini glass from a nearby cabinet and filled the glass to the brim.

"A twist?" she said, flashing Frank a quick smile.

"No, I prefer an olive or two."

"Very well." She handed him the drink while taking a sip of her own.

"Did you know the other two men on the aircraft with your husband?"

She looked puzzled for a moment, then suspicious. "What's that supposed to mean?"

"Nothing, really. I was only wondering if you had ever met them socially, like at a company party. Something like that."

Her expression slackened. She smiled over her glass, then laughed. "I should say I did." She said with emphasis, "And I can't say I'm sorry the son of a bitch died either. If there was ever a guy who deserved it, it's him."

"Who are you referring to?" Frank asked.

"That SOB Charles Rawlson, that's who. The other guy, Asbury, I didn't know."

She flopped down on the sofa and folded one leg under the other. "I may as well tell you. It doesn't make any difference now. It was one of those times when Tommy was on an extended trip for the company. I had met Charlie Rawlson before at some company function, or was it when I went to pick up Tommy at the airport . . . I don't remember now.

Anyway, Tommy was out of town at the time. I was bored out of my mind sitting around. Then Rawlson called and invited me to a party at his home, mostly company employees, he said. So I went. I didn't think there was any harm in it. When I got there, I didn't see anybody I recognized, but I convinced myself to stay. Besides, I like people and noise, and my God, there's nothing I hate more than to be alone. So, I had one drink after another. The next thing I knew, Rawlson and I ended up in a bedroom and, strangely enough, that seemed all right too. Then he saw me home like a perfect gentleman. Only I didn't know that creep had recorded our tryst. He called me the next day and played the recording over the phone."

"Blackmail?"

"No, nothing like that. He did it for kicks, for laughs. But you never knew with Rawlson. He was so far ahead of everyone else. It was like he had superhuman powers to predict what people were going to do before they did it. Not long after, when Tommy was flying, Rawlson showed up. He had somehow gotten a copy of my key card—must have been that same night he made the tape—and he just let himself in. I'm no dummy, Mr. Adams. What could I do?"

"Did Rawlson become a regular visitor when your husband was out of town?"

She finished her drink and immediately poured another. She had seemed perfectly sober only a few minutes ago, but the story had thrown a few switches in her brain, and she was becoming incoherent, fast.

"Soon, every time Tommy was out, Rawlson was there, ready for fun and games. He even brought a 'friend' with him once. And I remember thinking, 'A guy friend? This is getting way too kinky for me.' So, I said something. Not only that, 'the friend' was just too sleazy. Never saw him again."

Her eyes were half closed and slightly out of focus, the drink wavering precariously in her fingers. She looked straight at him.

"I don't want to talk about this anymore," she said. "I want my insurance money, and I want to get the hell out of this town. My God, all I do is want, but I never seem to get. You said you worked for NBST?" she slurred.

"Yes," Frank said.

"Then, tell me, when are they going to know something?"

"It usually takes about a year for the blue cover to get published."

"What the hell is a blue cover?"

"That's the official report of the investigation that includes the determination of probable cause."

"A year! A fucking year! You have got to be kidding me. That is so typical of the way government does things. Don't they know there are people out there who need answers now?"

Frank placed his drink on a nearby end table. He took a business card out of his coat pocket. "Here's another of my cards.

If you think of anything else, or if you just want to talk, my number is there. Okay? Put it somewhere safe." He placed the card in her free hand and folded her long, delicate fingers around it. "Thanks for the drink, and call if you want to talk."

She muttered something unintelligible. Shortly her mind would step into a black suspension of time, like a spinning wheel that had abruptly stopped. The drink would spill, and she would fall onto the sofa or the floor. Then, sometime in the morning, her mental circuit breakers would snap back in, and the wheels would start turning again. He knew all too well the terrible feeling of being bludgeoned unconscious by too much worry and too much alcohol.

He toyed with the idea of staying until the inevitable happened. He would have to take some of the blame if she hurt herself after he left. Her head lolled on the back of the sofa like a loose ball fastened to an elastic cord. The drink spilled on the arm of the sofa. He grabbed her glass and placed it next to his on the end table. Then he stretched her out on the sofa. She seemed less womanly and more like a sad teenager who had tried to take on the world of great, big adults and lost. She reeked of gin, cigarettes, and defeat.

He found a blanket in the bedroom and spread it over her. He would leave the lights on in case she woke up in the night. Night had already filled the picture window. The yellow and white lights of Washington winked in the dark like weak stars. That lighted phallus, the Washington Monument, stood out from the cluster of lights.

He quietly left Mrs. Green's apartment and signed out, looking again for a familiar name in the visitor logbook. But who would sign their own name for an illicit visit? He nodded to the security guard on the way out and was soon back on the street, away from the influence of the apartment building. He felt vulnerable.

He was in a section of the greater Washington area that he didn't know well, so he hurried to his car and almost involuntarily glanced over his shoulder.

He did not sleep much that night as he thought about the implications of Mrs. Green's confession. Jealousy was still a strong motive, even in this age of post-sexual liberation.

CHAPTER 7

February 13
Tuesday, 8:00 a.m.

Frank was at the office early that morning. Vickie burst into the office late, looking like a cross between the Michelin Man and a citizen of Nome, Alaska. He briefed her on the new job as she peeled away gloves, coat, boots, hat, scarves, and sweaters, all the while nodding with comprehension. Frank watched with amazement and admiration as Vickie dashed around the office going through her morning rituals: opening mail, making coffee, organizing papers, setting the thermostat, opening the blinds, checking the phone messages, and positioning her desktop computer just right.

When she was finally settled behind her desk, Frank said, "Mrs. Rawlson should be in sometime today to drop off some biographical information on her husband, and there are a couple things I want you to do. Find out what you can about her. You know, what her relationship was with her husband, any lovers, money troubles, or outside interests, and what she had to gain by his death. Also check out her parents, the same sort of thing. I want to know what kind of man Richard Russell is. His wife died recently, so see what you can find. Learn what you can about his firm—Amertek Electronics—any background you can dig up. Russell claims the son-in-law was special to him."

Vickie threw him a mock salute, her cute way of telling him that his instructions were approaching redundancy.

He laughed. "I'll call in a couple of hours. If anything really important comes up, I'll be at the NTSB, at Joe's office."

For the last six months, there had been security threats by several foreign terrorist groups against NTSB and FAA offices and officials. Both the NTSB and FAA had stricter security measures put into place. It was now necessary for Frank to check in with NTSB security, wait to be cleared for entry, and wait even longer for an escort.

When Frank finally made it to Joe's office, he found Joe sitting at his computer working on a report.

"Right on time," Joe said.

"As always!"

They climbed the stairs up to the lab, one flight up. The lab looked more like a college physics lab with instruments that analyzed and tested electronic equipment and metals. There were some chemical reagents for testing and analyzing plastics and fluids. The quiet was only interrupted by the hum of electronic equipment and sound of warm air rushing from the heating vent.

Joe spoke to a very serious-looking man in a white lab coat. The man listened, glanced at Frank, called in a woman, who was also in a white lab coat, and said something to her. She left quickly and returned a few minutes later with an eight-by-eight cardboard box. Joe opened it, thanked the two lab assistants, and motioned for Frank to move closer.

"Look at this. We got the instruments back from the manu-facturers, plus their reports."

Joe held up the exposed insides of an integrated gyro attitude indicator. He pointed to a series of wires that snaked to the contact brushes.

"You can see where parts of these brushes have apparently

shorted out. Three of the wires have shorted out and melted down to two-thirds of their length." He pointed to a blue insulated wire with the tip of his ballpoint pen. "But this wire is still intact. It looks like this system partially shorted out by a flaw in the housing. Maybe this?" He held up an instrument casing to the light. "You can see small gouge marks in the insulating lining of the instrument casing that correlate to the position of the shorted brushes. Assuming that the gouge marks were caused when the instrument was installed in its housing, it is possible that these brushes started electrically arcing some time back, gradually worsening until the instrument failed. But, for some reason, the instrument didn't show a warning flag. Possibly because there wasn't a complete electrical failure in the instrument. The pilot periodically received inaccurate altitude and pitch data, and with no warning flag, continued to make the wrong flight corrections. He believed the thing was still working. But by the time he realized what was happening—if he ever did—the bird had gone into overspeed and possible flutter, and that was that."

Frank examined the gouge marks, casing, and the complex working of the guidance system. "Couldn't the gouge marks have been caused by the plane's impact? The brushes could have been burned by something in the instrument itself, a piece of wire or something like that."

"Yes, that's been considered," Joe said. "But nothing foreign was found inside any of the guidance instruments, and the gouge marks aren't consistent with the rest of the impact damage. Plus, if there had been a broader electrical failure, the transponder would have gone out, which it did not." Then Joe pointed to a small coil of wire in the instrument casing. "The roll stop actuator would have engaged, which it also apparently did not."

"Interesting," Frank said. "Who makes this instrument?"

"Amertek Electronics. They have manufacturing plants in

Virginia and California, and their headquarters is here in Leesburg. They provide guidance systems for just about everybody: the military, the airlines, and private aviation as well. They're known for making the best systems around. This guidance system integrates navigation and control with guidance being the heart of the system."

Joe pointed to a mangled, charred instrument on the lab table. "This little baby collects data from navigation and control inputs and makes whatever adjustments are necessary to guide the plane to the target and adjust power and flight controls. They even use these things in ballistic missiles. The old inertial systems are far outdated. It would be hard to find one these days, although I've heard some companies in South America still use them. It's hard to believe Quality Control didn't catch something like this." He held up the burnt and bent instrument casing.

"What are the odds that the failure occurred in Amertek's own company jet, though?" said Frank. Then, as an afterthought, he added, "Do you know whether they sell their products to foreign governments?"

"Couldn't tell you. You'd have to talk to the big shots in the company, and one of them is quite dead."

"Could it have been sabotage?" Frank asked.

Joe looked at the chard instrument casing again. A brief look of puzzlement swept over his face, then disappeared. "I don't know. I doubt it. I guess it depends on what the saboteur wants. If he was targeting a specific person, it's pretty chancy. I mean, a saboteur wants to make sure he gets his mark. But with this kind of set up, the chances of getting the right man aren't good. Rigging an instrument like this takes some sophisticated know-how. Saboteurs still prefer bombs. Occasionally, one will know enough about airplanes to put something in the fuel or remove a part that will cause a malfunction on take-off. The pros depend on fire to destroy the evidence."

"Don't you think that could have been the plan here?"

Joe shrugged. "It could have been, but it's a hell of a lot easier to prove sabotage when you can find something. Gouge marks don't establish a thing. All the Board is going to have in this case is, at best, a not-so-plausible hypothesis. Something did go wrong with the guidance system on that airplane, but only God knows what and how."

"Wasn't this airplane certified for single pilot operation?" Frank asked.

"Yes, and the pilot, Mr. Green, had a spotless record. He consistently aced his performance checks and, from what we have gathered, was well liked and trusted."

Frank shook his head slowly. "If somebody did this, and I'm beginning to believe somebody did, I wonder whether he or she had any idea of the death and destruction they would cause."

Joe sighed. "In my experience, anyone who could do this doesn't give a damn about the consequences of what they do."

———

It was after lunch when Frank returned to his office. There was a ten-by-twelve-inch manila envelope on his desk. He pressed the Play button on his office recorder and heard Vickie's cheerful voice.

"Here is the stuff you wanted from Mrs. Rawlson. She was very prompt, and quite a dish too. Is this one pro bono boss?" Vickie giggled. "I'm sorry, I shouldn't say such things. Anyway, I'll be back around three. Oh, and I remembered to turn off the coffee maker, so it doesn't scorch. Love ya!"

Frank leaned back slowly in his chair, propped his feet on the desk, and opened the envelope. Inside were four-and-a-half typed pages, which read like a write-up in *Forbes* magazine.

Charles Rawlson, the good all-around boy from the clean and wholesome Midwest, pleased everybody all of his life, made all A's in grammar school and high school, was an Eagle Scout, President of the Honor Society, President of the Debating Club, President of the Future Businessmen of America Club, Vice President of the student body, and on and on until he went to Amherst in 1970 where he maintained a 3.8 GPA, majored in economics, and joined a good social fraternity. He joined Amertek Electronics, Inc. shortly after graduation, met and married the lovely Helen Russell, who was a senior at Smith at the time, and rocketed to the number-two position in the company.

The phone rang, jolting Frank. He picked it up.

"I hear you think somebody might have killed old Charlie," It was a male voice, use to giving commands.

Frank quickly engaged the recording system. "Who is calling?" he asked.

"Just one of his dear friends. Charlie had a lot of dear friends who wept with joy at the news of his departure from this life, and hopefully to one of everlasting torment in the next."

"Can I talk to you? Where are you?"

"I'm celebrating at the Paradise Lost. I've been celebrating all day. Come over and we can celebrate together. You'll get around to suspecting me sooner or later anyway. Look for me at one of the back tables. I'll be the one with the big grin."

Frank quickly gathered his things, including the recorder, and hurried to the subway station. He knew the place, one of those chic, overpriced establishments near Dupont Circle aimed at lawyers and business executives who still liked to think of themselves as college charmers.

He made good time and bounded up the long escalator at

Dupont Circle and quickly covered several blocks to Paradise Lost. He was discreetly ignored by the few customers in the place when he stepped into its smokey, tomb-like interior.

He walked toward the darker end. A man sitting alone at one of the highly varnished wooden tables motioned him over. Frank switched on the recorder in his pocket. As he approached, he could see that he was a handsome man in his late thirties, with manicured fingernails, which was always a red flag to Frank. He was clean-shaven, with perfectly trimmed and styled hair, including his eyebrows. Frank got the uncomfortable feeling that the man was staring at his crotch. *He's accustomed to depending on his appearance, always gambling on his first impression,* Frank thought. Even the way he stood up and allowed his blazer to fall open, exposing his cashmere wool vest, seemed timed and deliberate. His only flaw was a slight tremor as he extended his hand to Frank.

"Drink?" he said with a perfect oval smile that showed most of his gleaming white teeth.

"No, thank you," Frank said as he sat down across from him.

"I'll have another," he said to no one in particular, and signaled the waiter. "Name's Gerald Saunders."

Frank recognized it as one of the names Mr. Russell had mentioned. "One of Charles Rawlson's best friends and colleagues?" he asked.

"That would be stretching it a bit too much. I know who you are, Mr. Adams. Seems you have a reputation for a ninety percent success rate."

"Oh, how do you know?"

"My secretary did some checking."

"Then you must have known for some time about Mrs. Rawlson's concerns."

"Almost from the moment she dialed your number."

"May I ask how?"

Saunders flashed his college boy prankster's smile. "It's not what you might think, although I sometimes wish that it were. No, it was the old reliable executive grapevine."

"We all underpay our secretaries, don't we?" Frank said.

"Not me. I pay mine extremely well. Everybody knows about you, Mr. Adams. I only hope that the guy who did it found out that it worked and is now safely ensconced in Russia or some such horrible place."

"Well, Mr. Saunders, besides yourself, who do you think would want Rawlson dead?"

Saunders laughed, spilling a few drops of his drink onto his sweater. He immediately brushed away the drops and dabbed at the wet spots with a paper towel. "Everybody I know, and probably everybody who ever met him."

"Even his wife?"

Saunders looked straight at him. "Especially his wife," he said through tightened lips, "and nobody in the world would blame her."

The waiter brought Saunders's drink, placed it on the table, removed the empty glass, and vanished like a nocturnal bird. Saunders waved his hand in the air, simulating bird flight.

"Want to tell me why Mrs. Rawlson would want her husband dead?" Frank was curious about what he would say.

"I wish you'd have a drink; you know. That way I wouldn't feel so much like an oily snitch."

"It's a working day for me, and so far, I don't have anything to celebrate. But maybe when this is all over . . ."

Saunders laughed. "Yes, and I'm rooting for the bad guys." He took a long sip from the glass. "Charlie was the most corrupt, most satanic individual I've ever known, and I've known a truckload. You know, we business executives are stereotyped as being rather cold-blooded creatures, but Charlie belonged to a different class. I don't think he was above murder, rape, incest with his mother, or bestiality with a jackass. If he wanted something, he got it. There were no restraints, absolutely none. And it wasn't just in business matters. It was everything."

"Women?" Frank asked.

"Yes. If he wanted a woman . . . or a man, he got them. It didn't matter how. I didn't realize what was going on until—"

"Didn't anybody complain to Mr. Russell?" Frank injected.

"Are you kidding? They were blood brothers. Charlie was Russell's golden-haired boy, the son he never had. Someone tried it once. The last I heard he was still looking for a job as a shoeshine boy at Reagan National. It's the sort of thing colleagues try not to talk about."

"You said you didn't know what was going on until when, Mr. Saunders? Frank asked.

Saunders looked momentarily shaken. He took another long sip from his glass. Frank watched the laryngeal cartilage of Saunders's trachea work up and down amid a network of distended veins.

"One day we had lunch, and Charlie came out with it. He said, 'I want to go to bed with your partner, Doug.' It was like someone had hit me in the gut with a lead pipe. 'I wouldn't come right out and ask you this, old buddy,' he continued, 'but I've already given him a try, and he said no. Now I want you to see what you can do to persuade him.' Just like that, like it was some sort of business deal he wanted me to handle."

Saunders took another sip of his drink. "I've said enough," he said abruptly, "If you do discover that the son of a bitch was murdered, I can tell you there will be no shortage of suspects." The ice in his glass tinkled from his trembling hands.

"So, what did you do?" asked Frank.

Saunders sighed. "It's a terrible thing to live with one image of yourself, then to find out that image is nothing but a lie—something you created to help keep away the boogeyman. That comfortable little image I had of myself evaporated right then in a matter of seconds, and I saw things the way they really are. I was thirty-eight, with over a half-million dollars in debt, and less than a thousand bucks in savings. Charlie knew that, and he also knew that I am a gutless coward. So, I persuaded Doug, and he did it. He did it for me. Until last year. He left me a note with one word on it: goodbye. Haven't seen or heard from him since." Saunders's voice was shrill, like metal foil in the wind.

"If you wanted to make a confession, see a priest or a bartender or maybe a policeman. I can't forgive sins. I need facts, evidence. I have a job to do," Frank said.

Saunders lurched across the table, spilling his drink completely, and grabbed Frank by the collar. His eyes were red, and his mouth twisted. "Listen, you dummy. You're not going to solve anything. It's too big for you. You're a little man in a cage with a very large beast." He let go of Frank's shirt and settled back with a slight smile. "Even if you are lucky and can prove it was murder, you won't be able to pin it on anybody. Don't you see what I'm saying?"

There was a long silence. The two men stared at each other across the table like two wary but determined boxers.

"Tell you what," Saunders said. "I'll offer myself up as a human sacrifice. I'll take the blame for it. It's the least I can do for all of us victims." He fell back into his chair, laughing maniacally. "That is, if you can prove it was murder."

Frank pushed his chair back and stood up. "Sorry, but I don't take volunteers. As far as I'm concerned, if Rawlson was murdered, it was a crime and not a heroic act." He dropped his card on the table. "But if you come up with something concrete next time, call me."

He could hear Saunders's laughter as he walked out of the bar, and he believed he could hear it all the way to the Metro station. There had been something threatening in Saunders's tone and in his manner, and it gnawed at Frank for hours.

Vickie was at her desk when Frank returned to the office.

"Sorry, Boss. I couldn't find out much about the names you gave me. They all seem like a clean bunch—no police records, no tax problems. On paper, they look like saints."

"Yeah, well, the last saint died centuries ago, but thanks anyway. I'm beginning to think I may have taken on more than I can handle with this case."

Frank walked over to the window. Planes were taking off from Reagan National in sequences of three- to five-minute separations.

"I know there was a murder committed. The navigation system wasn't just defective; it was tampered with. And how many experts are there around here with that kind of skill and knowledge? That little voice that has saved my life a couple of times keeps whispering warnings. You know, like when you're in the presence of danger that isn't obvious or something that reeks of pure evil but you can't see it."

He turned away from the window. "Or maybe it's an overindulged ego refusing to give up. Or . . ." He stopped at the door to his office. "Maybe it's an intense fear of having to do auto accident cases for insurance companies."

Vickie did not laugh as he had expected her to.

"You'll work it out, Mr. Adams," she said earnestly.

She was trying to sound confident. It reminded him instantly of his high school math teacher encouraging him when there was nothing else left for her to do. Not quite emptied of hope, but not giving him much of a chance either.

"Vickie, I want you to do some real digging on this guy Gerald Saunders. Find out where he goes, if he has a history, who he sleeps with or doesn't sleep with. He strikes me as being on the edge."

Vickie nodded. "Sure thing, Boss, but it may take some time."

CHAPTER 8

February 14
Wednesday, noon

Sal finished the remainder of his cool rum gimlet and sat up to see his wife running up from the beach, her lovely body glistening like smooth, brown enamel. She seemed very happy with their new fortune and seemed to believe, without question, that it had been the forgotten inheritance of one of Sal's old aunts in New York.

Angela was a simple girl, and that was what he loved about her. She would have been just as content to live outside Washington in a cracker box suburb for the rest of her life. She was never ashamed of him, even when his electronics repair business failed and he had to go to court, or when he had to file Chapter 7. She stood with him, defended him to the wall, even against her own family. She truly believed that their recent good fortune was God's justice for the way they had been treated by the court.

Sal smiled. Perhaps she was right in a strange way. When the opportunity came to get even—he couldn't think of it without feeling a surge of anger—he took the chance and became $50,000 richer.

He placed the empty glass down on the table next to his lounge chair and signaled to the waiter for another. A gust of warm, scented wind rustled the dried palm leaves of the cabana roof. Angela ran up to him, rubbing her black hair with a towel, and kissed him on the cheek. The musk of her warm, salty human flesh enveloped him. He ran his hand along the smooth, tight skin of her leg.

"Oh, Sal, it's been a wonderful vacation, and the best Valentine's Day ever! The time has gone by so fast. It's such a shame it has to end."

She looked toward the shimmering beach and the distant bobbing of a Hobie Cat skimming over the blue water, its sail beating the air like a small white wing. She finished drying her hair, tossed the towel to the edge of the cabana, flopped onto the other bamboo lounge chair, and started brushing her hair straight back so that it conformed to the perfect shape of her head.

"Sweetheart," Sal said in his usual way that warned of more important things to come. She stopped brushing her hair and looked directly at him, wide eyed and receptive.

"We don't have to end it," he said. "This last month has just been a taste of what's to come. Don't ya see what's happened? We've had some really good luck. The kind they make movies about, you know. I mean, look."

He held up a three-day-old edition of *The Washington Post.* "Look at that, would ya? Nothing but freezing rain, ice, snow, and crime in the street. We don't have'ta put up with that anymore. If we sold the house and everything, we'd have enough money to do anything we wanted."

Angela looked puzzled, reluctant. "Sal, I don't know. What would we do? We can't play for the rest of our lives. And selling the house . . . I don't know. I think I'm against that."

"Listen, babe. Your problem is you've never been rich before. It's a whole new ball game. People listen to you when you're rich. Everybody just can't wait to do you favors. Wealth in America buys you respect and power."

"But fifty thousand dollars, plus what we could get for the

house and all, just doesn't sound very rich to me." Her face twisted with doubt. "Aren't you dreaming a little too big?"

"What do ya mean, too big? What do ya mean, huh? You don't know anything about business. I can take that money, put it in the stock market, and double it in a few months." Sal stood up and raised his right hand as though making a vow to the heavens. "There's lotsa ways to make money, but you gotta have money first. Now we got some, and I mean to pile it higher and deeper." Sal slapped the table with his hand.

"I'm sorry, Sal. I know you know more about these things than I do."

Sal grunted.

"But, I mean, it sounds like such a big risk to sell everything."

"Believe me, darlin'. Sal knows what he's doing," Sal said with a slight smile and an expression of supreme confidence.

The waiter brought Sal's drink and placed it on the table next to him, then nodded with a smile and quietly walked back to the hotel. Sal took a long sip of the rum gimlet, then leaned back on the soft cushions of the lounge chair, closed his eyes, and took a deep breath of the luxurious Caribbean air. His knowledge had finally paid off. Killing somebody was easy. Only the crazies got caught: the outraged husband blowing the balls off his wife's lover, or the maniac who barricaded himself in a house and opened fire on everybody in sight with an automatic rifle. As far as anyone knew, he had no reason to kill Charlie Rawlson. "I actually sort of liked him," Sal said quietly to himself, unable to resist a slight smile.

Sal thought about Rawlson. The man always had some new joke to tell him when he saw Sal at work. Someone wanted to get Rawlson out of the way, someone who knew Sal was hard pressed for cash and good with electronics. *It was business, that's all, and it was easy. You could get away with murder in this country. Nobody really gives a damn but steal their money and they'll hound you to the ends of the earth. They'll send an army after you. You can't get away with stealing as easily as you can with murder,* he thought.

Sal finished his gimlet, stood up, and stretched his rested body. "Let's go for a swim, honey," he said.

She smiled sweetly, like a pubescent girl.

"And don't worry, okay?"

"Okay," she said, taking his hand and walking with him down to the water.

They lingered at the bar after dinner. Sal was talking with a businessman from Miami about mineral and real estate investments.

Angela couldn't stop yawning. She covered her mouth with her fingers. "Sal, honey, I'm so tired after today. I hate to leave, but I really have to go back to the hotel."

"Sure, baby. Why don't you go ahead? I'll be along in a little while."

Sal and the businessman from Miami talked until after midnight. The man glanced at his watch and jumped up from the table, exclaiming that he had to go, that he wasn't aware of the time. He thrust his card at Sal and, not waiting for Sal to take it, let it drop in front of his face. Sal watched as the card fell to the table.

Sal grabbed the man's hand and shook it vigorously. Then he flopped back down in his chair, his mind dizzy with the seemingly endless financial proposals the man had offered. It was completely amazing. Money did seem to attract all kinds of opportunity. It had a magnetic force of its own. He had only been rich for a few weeks, and he already was going into international business.

He checked the man's business card again. There was a phone number on the back, but the name did not match the face. Sal thought the man was Middle Eastern. He had dark hair and a thin black mustache, and he spoke with an accent. Regardless of what name he was using, he was in the oil business, and Sal did not want to miss out on this chance.

Sal left the bar and stepped outside. He enjoyed the short walk to the hotel. He stopped in front of his hotel for a moment to breathe in the quiet, warm splendor of the tropical night. Suddenly, he felt something hard pressing into his back and then intense pain inside his head.

When he woke up, he felt pain. His head pounded in rhythm to an engine throbbing near him somewhere in the dark. The stench of rotting fish and diesel fuel made him retch. An intense white light exploded in his face. He squeezed his eyes shut, but the light still penetrated. He could feel its flameless heat on his skin.

"Ahhh, good evening, Coptin. So hoppy you could join us," a heavily accented voice said.

The light switched off. Hands grabbed him by the arms and shoulders and jerked him into a sitting position. He could see fading lights in the distance. Dim lights showed the half-silhouetted figure of a man in the pilot house of a boat. Salty spray swept over him occasionally, and he realized he was naked except for his underwear. The boat rolled and pitched. They were at sea, off the island. All he could think to say was, "What am I doing here?" He repeated it. "What am I doing here?"

A voice came out of the darkness. He had never been in such complete darkness. Except for the few distant lights, it was like the dark of a windowless room. He couldn't even see a reflection of light off the water. There were no stars, no sky, no water, and yet he was on a boat somewhere.

"A mon came to me and say dat he would like you to have swimming lessons. I am a good swimming teacher. I toll him I use the old ways: sink or swim. This he know, so he pay me well to teach you."

"Hey! Hey!" Sal heard himself yelling, but it didn't seem quite real. "What are you guys up to? What is this? Swim? I can't swim."

"Dis is what de mon say. So, I must teach you, he say."

More hands grabbed him and pulled him to his feet. He stumbled against the pitch and roll of the vessel, but the hands held him upright. They were powerful hands, more like great talons locked around his upper arms.

"We must part now, Coptin. Enjoy your swim, and if you make it to shore, you should try de English Channel next time."

The voice laughed in the throaty, thick way of the island natives and continued laughing as Sal was suddenly picked up and thrown.

For a moment he tumbled through the air like a free-falling parachutist. Then he hit the water, which felt and sounded like breaking glass. He never learned how to swim. He knew he was making all the mistakes of someone about to drown. He thrashed at the water, trying to crawl on top of it. He was breathing in short bursts.

He heard the boat speeding away and saw its red navigation lights as it turned. He caught a glimpse of the lights on the island. He started to crawl for those lights, but he was slowly pulled under by a soft, gentle, and a seemingly inescapable force.

He thrashed harder, but the water was now up to his chin and filling his mouth, snatching away the great breaths that his lungs groped for. He was going under. This was the end. He thought about the money and about the life he would not have, and in his rage, he cried out—not for help, or for God, or for his wife. His cry was one desperate last animal scream against death.

Black water closed over his face, shutting off the air. He hoped, vaguely, that he would be unconscious before the convulsions started. Air never seemed so precious before, just a simple breath of air. Some last spasm of will drove him upward as he clawed to the surface again. His hands broke free, grasping the air.

Then his left hand hit something hard. Instinctively his fingers closed on it, clutching it like a bird of prey. He pulled himself toward it. It was a half-submerged log that still smelled of pine and had no sea growth on it—probably fell off a lumber shipment to the island. Sal laid both arms over it and inhaled like a thirsty man gulping water. He rested his head on the log for a while. He could still die out here. There could be sharks, or he could lose his strength and slip away from the log.

But it was sharks he thought about now, gliding unseen in the black water, picking up his scent and moving in on him. If he could last until daylight, there was a good chance he would be picked up. He didn't want to take that chance.

He looked around. Whenever he floated up on the crest of a wave, he saw the bobbing lights of the island, but he lost sight of them when he slipped into the wave's trough. He thrashed and kicked until he was able to point the log in the direction of the lights. Then he dragged one free hand through the water, pulling himself forward. It would be slow progress, maybe even impossible, to drag the log with him, but he had to try. It was better than floating in the water like fish bait. As he pulled himself toward the island, he tried not to think about the sharks lurking in the depths.

The wind picked up during the night, changing direction and increasing in velocity. It drove him steadily toward shore. Even so, it was almost midday before he saw several men run down from the beach and splash out to help him ashore.

He had difficulty walking, so they carried him up to a metal-covered cabin near the beach. His skin was blistered, wrinkled in places, and white. He was covered in jellyfish sting welts. A Black woman doused his wounds with vinegar, wrapped him in a cotton blanket, and fed him fish broth that he couldn't keep down.

"I was out on a night cruise," he explained to the curious faces. The skin on his face burned, and it hurt to talk. "With some friends. To see the island at night. You know, the lights and all that. It was a kind of party before leaving the island, you know."

The faces remained uncomprehending except for their curious eyes.

"We were swimming off the boat," Sal continued, "and I guess I sort of got lost. You know, disoriented, with only a few lights to go by. You know how it is on a dark night. I bet you get this all the time with us crazy tourists, don't you?"

"You went swimming in your underwear, mon? That does sound crazy to me."

The woman approached again with her soup. "You have been in the water many hours, mon. You must take some food."

"Ah jeez, I appreciate it. I really do. You people have been really nice. I mean, where I come from, anybody seen me drifting onto the beach like that woulda searched me for valuables first. But really, I have'ta get back. My wife has probably got the Coast Guard out looking for me right now. Could one of you fellas give me a ride to the hotel? I'll pay you, of course."

Everyone crowded in the metal shack looked at one another. Then a large man with the dignity and bearing of a local chieftain stepped forward. "I am going into town. I shall take you to the hotel," said.

Sal warmly thanked his rescuers and followed the man to his truck, stepping like a barefoot tightrope walker on the rocky path.

On the way to Sal's hotel, he asked the man if he would also take him to the airport after he collected a few things from his hotel room. He told the man that his unforeseen accident had caused him to be delayed for a very important meeting back in the States. He was in a desperate hurry, he said. The man thought about it for a while. Then, just as the hotel came into view, he agreed.

"Ah, you American tourists. You come here to relax and lay in de sun, and still you always hurry. What a country America must be."

Sal told the man to park behind his hotel. He looked around carefully before getting out.

"I'll be back in a minute, okay?"

"Surely," the man said, smiling happily.

Sal slid out of the truck cab, looked around carefully, and walked slowly but casually to a grove of cedars and tall bushes near the truck. He pushed through the sharp-edged foliage as close to his hotel as he could and searched the open space between himself and the hotel window. It was clear.

He approached the window silently and peered in. Angela was alone and dressing. He tapped on the window. She looked up, startled, crossed her arms in the front of her body in an instinctive female defense posture, then threw her hands to her mouth when she recognized who it was.

Sal pointed frantically to the door. When he saw her start for it, he hurried to the corner of the building. There were people down on the beach and in a few in the nearest cabanas. He recognized them as hotel guests. They were all absorbed in conversation or shaking out sandy towels. He heard the door open.

"Wait," he hissed. "Wait."

When all the guests were turned away from him, he quickly darted around the corner and into the room, closing and locking the door behind him.

"My God, Sal! What happened to you last night? I've been—" She noticed his under shorts. "What are you doing in your underwear? Did you go swimming in your underwear at night? You can't swim, Sal. Oh, Jesus, Sal, you didn't . . . that woman at the bar . . . ?"

"Goddamit, will you shut up and listen!"

Sal raced around the room collecting his clothes from the closet and tossing them into his suitcase. He was trying to dress with one hand and pack with the other.

"I've got to get back to Washington in a hurry. My life depends on it. I need cash for traveling. How much have you got?"

Angela was in a state of shock, unable to move. Sal quickly zipped up his pants and tightened his belt. He grabbed her purse and dumped the contents on the top of a night table and spread it out with his hands.

"Is this all?" He held up fifty dollars in fives and tens. The bills wriggled in his hand like a group of small fish.

"I'm sorry, Sal. I just haven't gotten around to going to the bank yet. I'll run there now. They have an ATM machine."

"No, not now. There isn't time. I'll take the cash and your debit card."

He stuffed his wallet back into his pocket along with the fifty in cash.

"I want you to stay here for a couple more days. Lay out in the sun, have a good time, and don't worry about nothing. I'll be all right. Nobody should come around. They think I'm dead, but in case somebody shows up, for God's sake, don't tell 'em you ever saw me. If they ask you if I've turned up, you tell 'em no. Tell 'em I sometimes disappear for weeks at a time and that you never know when you'll see me. Okay, baby, okay?"

Angela's eyes were wide. "Sal, they think you're dead? What the hell is that all about, and who the hell is 'they'? It sounds like you're in some kind of real trouble this time."

"Yes." He patted her cheek gently. "But I'll be all right; I'm always all right. You know that, baby, don't you? Don't worry about a thing, I'm going to Washington to get it all straightened out. I'll call you in a few days. Okay?"

She nodded. Small tears started to run down her cheeks.

"Hey, don't do that now," Sal said, gently touching her face.

"But I'm scared, Sal. I'm really scared this time."

"There's nothin' to be scared of, darling. There's all that money in the bank."

"Sure," she said as tears dripped from her chin. "What good is all that when—"

"It's gonna be all right, I'm tellin' you. Now, for Christ's sake, stop crying. I gotta go!" Sal hesitated for a moment as he reached the door. He looked back at Angela.

"You're right, honey. Fifty thousand ain't rich. I'll get us some more that'll make us rich." With that, he grabbed Angela's huge sunglasses and floppy sun hat off the bed and kissed her.

"Sal!"

But that was all he heard as he slipped out the door, around the hotel, and back along the cedar grove to the big man's truck. He hopped into the truck with childlike nimbleness and said, "Okay, buddy. Now if you could give me a lift to the airport, there's twenty-five big ones in it for you."

CHAPTER 9

It seemed everyone at the management level, and most of the employees, had a motive to kill Charles Rawlson. Almost no one expressed regret at Rawlson's fate, and several even hoped that the murderer—if there was one—would escape. But Frank was beginning to doubt that Rawlson had been murdered. Sabotaging the guidance system was simply too sophisticated to be credible. It was an accident so freakish, so statistically remote, that the sheer likelihood of elements coming together perfectly for that failure moment seemed ridiculous.

There was also the reality that few of the people who disliked Rawlson enough to kill him also had the know-how. They were mostly executive types with MBAs, and although Vickie's background check on these company executives revealed that most of them had bachelor's degrees in engineering, none had ever worked in a specialized field like aircraft guidance systems. The electronics industry was so specialized that each component had its own expert. There were experts in twelve-volt capacitors or twenty-amp fuses. Some of the company employees were horrified at the thought of a complete guidance system expert running around loose. They believed that whoever tampered with the system, if someone actually did, had to come from outside Amertek Electronics. For a brief moment, Frank wondered whether the pilot or the other passenger had been the target. He dismissed the idea that the pilot, Green, was the target of murder. From what he had learned, Green had no enemies, with the possible exception of his wife, who struck Frank as not having it together enough to make a ham sandwich.

What about the other passenger, Mark Asbury? He was a junior officer who was acting as witness and to take notes. In the defense industry, it was always wise to have third-party observers to keep records.

Frank leaned back in his desk chair and asked Vickie about the small stack of annual reports and stock tip sheets she had assembled.

Vickie moved a little closer to Frank as if she was about to whisper something in his ear. "By the way, I have a friend who has a friend at Amertek, and she tells me that there is some strange stuff going on there."

"In what way?" Frank asked.

"It's just that things and people may not be what you see. I need some more details, so ask me later."

Frank nodded. "Let's be careful about trusting office gossip. However, you're right in that there's often something solid at the core of gossip. See what you can find out from your friend and verify as much as possible."

Vickie nodded. "I also read through the reports and share tip sheets and noticed that Amertek's sales and profits in the previous fiscal year stayed steady until the last quarter when the share price plummeted. Apparently, there was a failed merger that upset the market. There was a leveling-off period at the end of the last quarter, but only a few weeks ago, Amertek's shares went up and have been on a steady rise. The latest earnings report is not yet available, but there was a note at the bottom of the last page. Amertek had signed a ten-million-dollar contract with a

London-based company for classified electronic equipment. Its sales to private companies, foreign and domestic, had increased twenty percent."

The phone rang. Vickie ran to her desk to answer it.

"It's Mrs. Rawlson," Vickie announced over the intercom.

Frank picked up the phone.

"I got a call just now from a man who claims to know something about Charles's death," Mrs. Rawlson said. "He wants one hundred thousand dollars. He said he knows who the murderer is, but he wants to be paid." Mrs. Rawlson sounded uncharacteristically rattled.

"Did you get a name?" Frank asked.

"He refused to give it. He wants to meet me."

"Where?"

"In a parking lot near the old Torpedo Factory, tonight. I'm leaving now."

"Wait right there, I'll be over," Frank said.

"He wants me to come alone. He insisted."

"They all insist, but this is the first real break we've had, Mrs. Rawlson, and without it I've got nothing but dead ends. Now listen. Use the biggest car you have. Pull up at the Exxon gas station on the corner of Van Dorn and Seminary Road. Fill the car up with gas, then drive around to the restrooms on the right side of the building. Go into the restroom and make sure you leave the car doors unlocked. The gas station will be on the right, so there will not be a problem. Be there at 5:30 exactly."

"Yes, but I don't like it. I really don't. What if he sees us?"

"He won't see us, believe me. Whoever he is, he wants to get in, get the money, and get out fast."

"Well, all right, but I'm really nervous about this. It's starting to become serious. Don't you think we should inform the police?"

"Mrs. Rawlson, the NTSB has probably listed your husband's

death as 'undetermined.' It's only a routine police matter. It would take too long to bring them in, and you can bet the first thing they would do is scare this guy off. Then again, this may be a hoax—some guy heard about the investigation and sees an opportunity for a fast buck."

"All right. I'll do as you ask, but I'm still nervous about it."

"Don't worry," Frank said and hung up.

Frank was nervous too. A clandestine interception was always tricky and occasionally deadly.

He loaded a clean tape into the mini recorder, checked the batteries, then placed it carefully into his side pocket, took a deep breath, and left for the gas station.

Frank parked in the shadows at the back of the small, paved station lot. He knew the layout well. He waited until he heard Mrs. Rawlson's car drive up, then gave her a few minutes to get gas before getting out of his car and walking toward the men's restroom. While in the men's room, he heard the door to the women's restroom open and close. He stepped outside, waited behind the partition for several car headlights to flash by, then walked low and quickly around to the shadowed side of a Fleetwood Brougham. He opened the back door just enough to slip into the back seat. Frank closed the door quietly and lay on the floor, surprised at how rapidly he was breathing. He held the tape recorder in his hand. He would hate to have to explain this if anyone saw him.

Mrs. Rawlson exited the restroom, got back into the driver's seat, shifted the lever into drive, and rolled back out onto the street.

Frank could tell it was going to be an uncomfortable ride. He cleared his throat and said, "I'm in the back seat. Play the radio. Loud."

She yelped. The car swerved. She slammed on the brakes, and Frank thumped into the back of the front seat. The car came to a halt, engine running. She took a few audible deep breaths and switched on the radio: a Mozart piano concerto.

"Keep going, Mrs. Rawlson," Frank said in an urgent whisper.

"You nearly scared me to death." Mrs. Rawlson's voice sounded an octave higher than normal. "You should have told me what you were up to."

"There's no time for that now. I'm sorry, but it was the only way I could do it and keep you reasonably safe."

"Do you think he's bugged the car?"

"If he's the guy who can bring down a sophisticated jet, then it's a possibility."

The big Cadillac started moving again. Streetlights flashed by the windows. Car headlights flashed and illuminated the car ceiling with moving, irregular patterns.

"What are you going to do?" Mrs. Rawlson asked.

"Be reasonable with him. Convince him that he can trust me."

"Do you think this man killed my husband?" Her voice quavered a little.

"I don't know, but it's beginning to look like somebody did."

Mrs. Rawlson made several turns. The streetlights became fewer.

"Okay, Mr. Adams. We're at the parking lot where he told me to meet him."

"Do you see anything?" Frank asked, slipping his hand into his coat to switch on the tape recorder.

There was a long moment of silence.

"No, not even another car."

Then the rear door swung open with a metallic crack. A small man jumped into the back and pressed a gun barrel against the nape of Frank's neck. Frank's entire body stiffened.

"I'm not playing games here," the man said, but his voice was muffled, as if he was holding one hand over his mouth. "You didn't follow my instructions, Mrs. Rawlson. Do you want me to convince you of that?"

"No, please!" she said, holding her hands up. "He's just a private consultant. He has nothing to do with the police. I hired him to substantiate my insurance claim."

"Lady, I don't have time for lies."

"But she's not . . ." Frank began.

The man jabbed the muzzle into the base of Frank's skull. "Hey, buddy. If you don't shut up, I'm going to take your head off at the base."

"Okay, okay, but I'm not going to hurt you," Frank insisted.

"You got it backwards, friend. I'm going to hurt *you* if you don't keep your mouth shut and keep looking straight at the floor. Now," the man said to Mrs. Rawlson, "you got the money?"

"You . . . you didn't say to bring the money," Mrs. Rawlson stammered in a high-pitched voice.

"Lady, what in the name of Christ did you think this meeting was all about?"

"I thought you wanted to give me your information first, and then I would pay you. I could write you a check right now. Would that be acceptable?"

"It seems, Mrs. Rawlson, that you don't know how this game is played. Writing me a check is the last thing I want you to do."

He turned. "It's a pity you didn't keep your side of the bargain. You should have done what I told you, lady." He nudged Frank with the barrel of his gun. "He says he's not a cop, but everybody's a cop to me. I will tell you this much: your husband was murdered.

It was a contract killing. Take my word for it, but it's much bigger than both of you. You two could both disappear, and although there'd be plenty of questions, there'd be no answers."

Frank felt the barrel of the gun press harder into his neck.

"I'm leaving now," the man snapped. "If either of you makes a move or even looks back, my partner is watching down the barrel of a silenced twenty-two with hard point bullets. So don't get any ideas about following. Just stay put for fifteen minutes, no less. Got that?"

Frank and Mrs. Rawlson both nodded.

The back door opened, the man stepped out, closed the door quietly and disappeared.

"Aren't you even going after him? He is obviously bluffing," Mrs. Rawlson said almost shrieking.

"Did you not hear what he said? If you want to call his bluff, then be my guest, but I'm going after him on more favorable ground!" Frank shouted. Then, in a more moderate tone, he asked, "Did you recognize the voice?"

"I don't know." Mrs. Rawlson seemed to be on the edge of tears.

Frank rewound the tape and played it back. The conversation was surprisingly clear.

"Well, do you?"

"No, I thought . . . but no, I don't recognize the voice."

Frank slumped down in his seat and exhaled slowly like a balloon deflating. "Mrs. Rawlson, would you mind driving me back to my car?"

Mrs. Rawlson glared at him then angrily snapped the gear shift handle into drive, and sped away, leaving a thin smoke trail of burned rubber.

CHAPTER 10

February 16
Friday, 9:00 a.m.

Frank decided to play a hunch based on information that Vickie had dug up, and he wanted to see Saunders's reaction. He pulled into the parking lot of Amertek Electronics a little after nine the next morning. He parked in a visitor parking space, marked yellow, close to the main entrance. He walked gingerly on the newly sanded ice-coated walkway. Saunders's office assistant looked at him with an early morning poker face, pinched red from the cold.

"Do you have an appointment?" She glanced at his business card.

"No, just tell him Frank Adams needs to see him."

She appeared slightly amused but restrained her flickering smile. She picked up the inter-office phone and pressed a button. "Mr. Saunders, a Mr. Frank Adams says he needs to see you. He's a private consultant."

She listened for a moment. Her expression became more serious. "Mr. Saunders will see you now," she said with studied disinterest.

Frank thanked her and walked down a short hallway to Mr. Saunders's office. He opened the naturally finished oak doors and stepped inside.

Saunders was standing by his desk looking through some papers. He looked up, then took a few steps toward him, and greeted Frank with an extended hand.

"Awfully sorry about the last time we talked," he said.

"Are you?" Frank asked.

"You know, too much to drink, the business adjusting to Charlie's death, all of that." He motioned Frank to a chair in front of his desk. "Please, have a seat."

Frank settled comfortably in the plush chair, crossed his legs, and waited for the next move. Saunders fidgeted clumsily with some material on his desk—placing objects in a precise order, arranging pens according to size, and stacking papers squarely together. There were photos hanging on the wall of him accepting sports trophies, civic awards, and one photo of him as Henry IV in a local theater production. There were several photos of a young man on his desk, facing him, unlike many business executives and politicians who preferred to have pictures of their families facing the visitor.

"What can I do for you, Mr. Adams?" he finally asked, reestablishing his wide, oval smile.

Frank reached into his coat pocket and pulled out his mini tape recorder. "Do you know what this is?"

Saunders looked puzzled, raising his eyebrows a bit too theatrically. "Of course. It's an old-fashioned, out-of-date mini recorder. I don't get it."

"Listen," Frank said, and he pressed the Play button.

Saunders listened to the tape without a single change of expression.

"That's very interesting, Mr. Adams, but don't you have the wrong address? Shouldn't you be at the police station with that instead of here?"

"Do you recognize the voice?"

Saunders shook his head. "No."

"You should. It's one of your employees."

Saunders wrinkled his brow as though taking aim at a target. "And why do you think that?"

"You know, Gerry, it really is a small world in spite of the billions of people in it. A lot of these people know one another, like my secretary, who knows one of your people. This person tells my secretary that one of your employees, Salvatore Sassavitte, used to be an electronics guidance systems technician. Sassavitte got into some trouble with the company he used to work for, and they let him go. He came to work for your outfit a couple of years ago as a bench worker until last November. Then, miraculously, he's promoted to a responsible job in quality control. That's your department, isn't it, Gerry?"

Saunders nodded. "So?"

"And you don't recognize the voice?"

"I've told you that I do not. No! Mr. Adams. There are over a hundred people in my department. I know them on the basis of progress and evaluation reports, not by the sound of their voices. Sassavitte had been a model worker. I was aware of his background. I thought his skills were being wasted, and I thought he deserved a chance."

"What puzzles me, though, is why he quit a month ago, just when everything was going for him," Frank said.

"Better opportunity, I suppose."

"Do you know where?"

"Our employees aren't required to give us any reason at all if they want to move on. Have you thought of asking Sassavitte himself?" Saunders said, making the contempt in his voice clear.

"The neighbors say he hasn't been home in weeks," Frank said.

"Sorry. Wish I could help you," Saunders said, his voice sharp and clear. He wanted the interview to end.

"You can help me," Frank answered.

Saunders glared at him.

"I want to talk with anyone who worked with Sassavitte."

"Mr. Adams, you are not law enforcement, and so far as I know, you're not even a licensed investigator. Essentially, you have no legal standing here, and as such, I'm under no obligation to permit you anything. However," Saunders put his hands together with his fingers pointed out, letting his index fingers touch his lips, "in the interest of fairness and cooperation, and since I know you have the support of the grieving widow and her father, you can do whatever you like. But I would prefer that you do it outside working hours. I would also appreciate it if you have accusations to make, you make them to the police and not to our employees. I can't see that it would do any good to falsely implicate one of our current or former employees in what could be construed as a blackmail attempt."

Frank stood up, noting that Saunders seemed unnerved despite his bravado.

"Okay, but I'll need the names of the people who worked closest with Sassavitte."

Saunders picked up the phone. "Doris, get me a list of the people in QC, Section 2, will you, please? Thanks."

He put down the phone and glared at Frank. "Mr. Adams, I should tell you that we're a close-knit group at Amertek Electronics. If you hurt one of our people needlessly, we will make you pay for it."

"I'll try not to hurt anyone, Gerry, whether they need it or not. But if you think threatening will scare me, then you're on the wrong track." Frank reached into his jacket pocket and pulled out his investigator's license and showed it to Saunders. "You're right, I'm not law enforcement, but this gives me legal standing and the right, under the laws of Virginia, Maryland, and the District of Columbia, to investigate."

Saunders's office assistant entered cautiously with a sheet of paper in her hand. She handed it to Saunders across the desk, glanced at Frank as if he might have a contagious disease, and left.

Saunders ran his eyes down the paper, then pushed it toward Frank. It was a list of Amertek employees in Quality Control along with their title, section, and shift.

"Say, Adams. I thought you investigated aircraft accidents. I didn't know you played cops and robbers too."

The remark was thick with sarcasm.

"I don't play at being a cop," replied Frank, "but when somebody shoves a gun in my neck and threatens to blow a hole through it, I tend to get personally involved and step outside my normal bounds."

"Just don't overstep them too much," Saunders warned in a menacing tone.

CHAPTER 11

February 19
Monday, 6:00 p.m.

Sal waited in his Virginia motel room until dark before heading to his house. He wasn't sure who was trying to kill him, but they probably wouldn't be watching the place since the fishing boat captain had, no doubt, reported him safely disposed of. In a few days, his wife would report him missing to the local police. After that, any surveillance on her would stop, and she'd be safe. Even if the fishermen had learned of his escape through the local grapevine, they would have a powerful incentive to keep their mouths shut and enjoy the money.

He thought about Angela. She'd be safe if they thought he was dead, and the less she knew, the better. He looked at his watch. Rush hour would be winding down soon, but there would still be a lot of activity on the streets to cover his movements, and it was dark too. He crushed out his half-smoked cigarette in an overflowing ashtray next to the bed and slipped on his old Air Force flight jacket, which still had faded impressions of Air Force insignia.

He drove south through the Dulles corridor. At this hour, most of the traffic on 28 was heading out from the beltway. He arrived in Centerville and parked in a fast-food parking lot. He turned and walked casually down the service road behind his and his neighbor's house. Most people were already home. He could see the kitchen lights on and harried wives bustling around their kitchens preparing the evening meal.

He stopped at the corner of his back fence and surveyed his property. It was totally dark, nothing unusual. No cars in the driveway, no barking dogs. He had not seen many cars parked on the main street either, but he still waited a little longer.

Cautiously, he opened the back gate and moved slowly into the yard. A thin coating of fresh snow crunched under each step. He planned to enter through the side door of the garage so he would not have to climb the back stairs.

The lock was frozen. He jiggled the key, but it wouldn't budge. He did not want to risk heating up the key with a pocket lighter, so he pressed his mouth against the cold brass metal of the lock and exhaled. His breath added enough heat and the lock turned. He slipped inside and eased the door closed behind him.

He felt his way along the wall of the garage to the door to the utility room, grabbing the emergency flashlight off the shelf while avoiding potentially noisy obstacles. He bumped and stumbled upstairs to the bedroom where he kept his important papers. He looked around quickly, felt for the drawer, opened it, and switched on the flashlight. All of his papers were there: bank account, titles, insurance policies, everything untouched just as he had left them. They hadn't even bothered to see if he was home. They knew where he was or where he should be.

Sal switched off the flashlight, stuffed the papers into his jacket pocket, and went back to the garage. His heart throbbed as he exited the side door of the garage. He felt as if all the vital metabolic heat was sucked out of his body. He was faint and shivered as he slipped through the doorway and stepped outside.

He closed the door gently but did not hear the click of the lockset. The lock had refrozen. He put his mouth against it to blow, but then something pressed into the center of his back, and a voice whispered in his ear, "Sal, I've been waiting out in the cold for a long time to see you. Please don't do anything rash."

Sal felt the muscles in his legs go flaccid and his knees thudded painfully against the frozen ground. He tried to speak, but his voice had gone too.

"Sal, Sal, I'm not going to hurt you. Even though I should after the way you treated me the last time we met."

"Hey! Hey! Who are you? What is this?" Sal rasped.

"I just want to talk this time. I think you need protection. My advice is to come with me."

Sal felt his strength returning. He sensed he was not in danger from this man. He felt the object removed from his back.

"Please, stand up, Sal. I only want to talk."

Sal got to his feet and turned around slowly. He could not see the man's face, but he could make out the silhouette of a well-dressed man of average height and build. He thought he recognized the voice.

"Who are you?" Sal repeated.

"Frank Adams."

"The guy in the car with Mrs. Rawlson?" Sal asked.

"That's right."

"Jeez, how'd you find me? What do you want?"

"The first question is not important, is it, Sal? But the second one is. I want to talk about the crash last month of the Amertek Electronics' company plane."

"Hey, I didn't have nothing to do with that."

"But you know something about it, don't you, Sal? They know you know something about it too. You're on the run, trying to extort money from Mrs. Rawlson, and trying to get them off your back. You didn't expect that, did you? Trying to figure out what's going on. And here you are, sneaking around your own place in the dark like a common burglar."

"Sorry, buddy," Sal said, "but we've got nothing to talk about."

"Now, as I said, I'm not a cop, only a private citizen like yourself. I can go to the police and tell them what I know. That'll give you a few hours of lead time. Or we can talk, and by the time all the facts are in, it may be as much as a month before I have to go to the police."

Sal grabbed Frank by his coat collar and shook him. "You know, you're in a dangerous position."

Frank easily pulled Sal's hands away from his collar. "I have insurance," he said, rustling his hand in his pocket to suggest a weapon. "And I know how to use it."

Sal glanced around in the snowy darkness. Lights twinkled in bright winter clarity from his neighbors' houses. They were alone. A gust of wind stirred wisps of snow around their feet. A shower of sparkling ice crystals from a denuded cherry tree blew by their faces.

"It wasn't a big thing . . . at first," Sal said as if he were in a confessional.

Frank stamped his feet and blew warm air into his hands. "First of all, let's get inside out of this frigid cold."

Once inside, still in the dark, Sal began to speak. "Until a few years ago, I used to work for Collier Instruments. Some people in the company saw me as a threat. I was good at my job—maybe too good. I always had a knack for math and electronic gadgets. I was on my way up, but there were people in the company— snobby, ivy league types—who saw me as a threat to their little club. Afraid I was moving past them. And they weren't going to have some little high school Air Force electronics techie bossing them around. So, they got rid of me.

"After that I went to work for Amertek. One day, my boss, Mr. Saunders, came up to me and asked me all about Collier gyro systems. It's a highly competitive business, avionics and instruments. He wanted priority information. I had to stay in his good books, so I told him everything I knew."

"Didn't you sign a non-disclosure agreement when you joined Collier?" Frank asked.

"What if I did? What did I owe Collier after the way they treated me? What choice did I really have? There aren't a million places to work in my field, and Saunders was my new boss."

"My assistant has been doing some digging, and she discovered that you were kicked out of Collier because you were stealing their industrial secrets and fencing them on your own," Frank said.

"Hey, hold on. Yes, I took some documents with me when I left Collier . . . just for insurance. But Saunders found out somehow and started threatening me. He threatened to turn me in for stealing proprietary information. Then he started pressuring me. He wanted me to do a special job for him, but it was top secret. There would even be a promotion in it for me— some real responsibility. So, I wrote this phony lab report for him, claiming that a bunch of parts of their latest system were defective. I thought we were good, but all hell broke loose when the report came out. The company lost a big client, and the share price went way down. I figured Saunders was nothing but a big-shot SOB—they all are—and he would bring the heat down on me. I decided to get out of there while the gettin' was good. So, I quit. I don't know why Saunders wanted that phony report. I can't see that he had anything to gain by it."

Frank said, "Nobody will believe you weren't involved in the crash of that jet. And now they've got you on the run."

"As far as the job on the Citation goes, one day I get this call. This fella with a pretty strong accent wanted to meet. He promised to make it worth my while. Everything was done by phone or in the dark with people I never seen before."

"Where?"

"I don't know. I met this one guy somewhere out on Mount Vernon Parkway, one of those scenic pull-offs."

"Did you recognize him?"

"No, it was night. He was heavily dressed, and like I said, he spoke in some kinda accent."

"Did you recognize the accent?"

"No. How should I know? They all sound the same to me. Anyways, this guy offers me fifty thousand dollars to knock off Rawlson and make it look like an accident. He offered me some upfront money to cover expenses and told me the plane would be left unlocked. How often does that kind of money come along? I knew Rawlson flew around in the company plane a lot, so I agreed."

"Why you?"

Sal shrugged, "I don't know. I'm smart with that stuff. Maybe they thought I don't got no principals. Maybe they thought I was a schmuck. But I got principals and I'm not a schmuck! Maybe they heard my prayers." He laughed like a teenager caught stealing tires. "So, I rented a van, dressed up like a high-priced lawyer, and went out to the airport. It was a clean job. I didn't leave a trace. And now, somebody tries to finish me off a few days ago. I don't get it," Sal said.

"Maybe they don't want any loose ends," Frank said. "Do you have an idea about who and why somebody would want to kill Rawlson?"

"Just about everybody I know at that place. Most people thought he was a real son of a bitch. Why don't you let it go? The world is a lot better off without that bum."

"And what about that performance the other night in Mrs. Rawlson's car?" Frank said.

"I was just trying to pick up a few more bucks from the

bereaved widow, that's all. I have to find out who's after me and why, and that's gonna cost me. I'm not touching my little nest egg."

"What about Saunders? He's got plenty of motive."

"Saunders! Ha, that's a laugh. He ain't got the balls to have a man killed. I mean it, everybody knows about him."

Sal jerked his head around and peered out the window as if he had heard a noise. "Listen, buddy, I gotta go."

"As I said before, I think you need protection. I have a little getaway cabin in the woods. It's warm and stocked with food. You'll be as safe there as you would be in California." Frank motioned toward the door.

"No thanks."

"But if there is a high-priced hitman out there with big money behind him, he's going to find you. Especially if there's another country involved, Sal. You know that."

Sal rubbed his chin with the back of his hand. "No worries. Big Sal's got a plan. I'm not as stupid as they think. I've got somthin' going." He paused. "But who wants to get me? I can't figure it out."

"I think it's the guys who paid you to do the job on Rawlson."

"But that doesn't make any sense. I did the job. They're off the hook. And I got lost. I went to the islands with my wife, for God's sake. And, besides, they've already paid me."

"You see, Sal, they're not off the hook as long as you're alive. They paid you knowing you would take off to some exotic place, and that's where they planned to do away with you. You would just be another American tourist killed in a boating accident or something like that."

"Boating accident. That's funny. That's exactly what they tried. But what about the money? Would they just throw away fifty thousand dollars?"

"Fifty thousand is peanuts to them. Of course, they could be planning on getting it out of your wife. I doubt she is safe from all of this." Frank continued, "They'll be watching your rented car and the street. It's too dark back here to see anything, at least with the naked eye. They know that you'll eventually have to move into the light."

Sal nodded. "Maybe you're right. They expect me to hop on the nearest plane and get as far away as I can. Maybe they wouldn't think to look for me around here, at least not for a while. And my wife's probably safe as long as I don't contact her."

Sal was silent for a moment, as his breath started to regulate. "Okay, I'll come, but first . . ." He slipped a hand into his jacket pocket, pulled out a .38 caliber Chief's special, and pushed it into Frank's lower rib.

"Move your hands out, away from your sides," Sal demanded.

Frank did as he was ordered. Sal kept the gun pressed hard against Frank's ribs and ran his free hand inside Frank's overcoat and along his body, stopping at the hard, flat lump in his coat lining. He reached for the concealed pocket opening and pulled out the mini tape recorder and examined it with his flashlight.

Sal smiled. "Well, at least it's not a gun." He held up the recorder. "So, what do you call this?"

Frank shrugged. "Evidence."

"So that's your game," Sal spit the words out like hot pellets. "I should waste you right here. What do I have to lose, huh?"

"Nothing, Sal. You're going to get it anyway. There is no place you can hide for long, you know that. One day you're going to be coming through a door and get blown away, just like that. And then they will probably take out your wife just to complete the job. Your only protection, Sal, is the law."

Sal pressed the rewind button on the pocket recorder and waited until the tape ran out. Then he pressed erase.

"Without this, you don't got nothin'." Sal put the recorder in his jacket pocket. "I'll take my chances. I'm not about to spend the rest of my life in a federal prison. Now, let's get up to this love shack of yours."

Frank maneuvered his tired, old Chevrolet onto Washington's suicidal beltway, staying in the outside lane. Cars, trucks, and motorcycles honked and thundered past him.

"Can't you move this heap any faster? Christ!" Sal snapped.

"I'm doing the speed limit, Sal. You want us to get stopped for a moving violation?"

Sal pretended to ignore the comment and looked nervously out the rear window. "Nobody else seems to be worried about it. Where the hell are all these people going at this hour?" he asked, releasing his hold on the pistol. Frank could sense Sal was tired.

Frank took an exit heading west. "Not the fastest way," he explained, "but more difficult for someone to follow."

Sal seemed to relax. "I don't know what I'm worried about. They think I'm dead." He laughed, hesitantly at first, but there was an undertone of hysteria to it.

"Yes, but eventually they'll find out that you're not. What then?"

Sal nodded. "Yeah, yeah," he seemed to be talking to himself. "There are the locals who helped me out, and one drove me to the airport. They thought I was just another dumb tourist who washed up on the beach. They've probably blabbed it all over the place by now. And there was that guy with the truck. He must have known something was funny."

Sal fell silent and slouched down in the seat. He looked like a teenage truant from a 1950s movie riding around looking for kicks. Occasionally he would sigh and wipe his face with his hand, then mutter something unintelligible.

Frank glanced over at him. It was hard to imagine that the rather ordinary looking man next to him had confessed to a calculated, cold-blooded killing without the slightest indication of remorse, even for the innocent victims of his act. Frank told himself that the protection he was offering this man was merely to gather information before he was finished off by the bad guys. He was taking a chance by taking him to his special retreat where he'd never taken anyone, but this was business, not social.

They were into the hills before Sal spoke again. "I've been thinking. You might be right about them catching up with me sooner or later, and money don't do you any good when you're dead. I mean, nothing does you any good then, does it? If I get a good lawyer and go to the cops and tell them everything, I could probably get a lighter sentence. Don't you think?"

"Say they coerced you," Frank suggested.

"Yeah, I was pressured."

"Yes, by a direct superior." Frank knew this wouldn't help him, but he wanted to reassure Sal to keep him calm. There was another alternative that Frank began to consider. Since Sal had confessed to a murder, he could easily wait until they reached the cabin. Then do away with him. No one would ever find the body. Sal could steal his car and make a run for it. There was no record of the confession, no witnesses. He knew that Sal was a desperate man grabbing at anything that looked like hope.

"It's the one advantage I've got over them," Sal was saying. "They expected me to run, even counted on it, and so far, I've done exactly what they thought I would do, except for not getting killed. How much farther to your place?"

"Only about ten miles on this road."

There was a long hesitation. Sal scratched his chin. "Okay, take me back. Let's go to the nearest police station. We can call the feds from there."

"What!" Frank yelled. This was completely unexpected. It didn't fit with Frank's plan, but he didn't have much of a choice now.

"You can't be serious," Frank said.

"I am, very serious. You are right. I'll be a hunted man for the rest of my life, and God knows what that will do to my wife. I think I would be better off in jail than always looking over my shoulder or checking for bombs, and hey, maybe I can take some of those rich bastards to jail with me."

Frank came to a slow stop on the narrow dirt and gravel track. Turning around would be difficult. The road was ankle-deep in muddy slush and ice, but he stopped and started to turn around. Saplings lining the road brushed his front and rear bumpers as he made small ten degree turns until, finally, by scraping his right bumper against a remaining fully grown tree, he could complete the turn and start back for Washington.

Almost immediately they were met by a pair of fast-moving headlights, jumping and swaying up the narrow road.

"What the hell's he up to?" Sal shouted. "Some drunk hillbilly. Let him have all the road he wants."

"I can't. There's no room," said Frank. "There's a pullover a mile or so behind. I can reverse back to it."

But the lights came to a sudden stop about a hundred feet from their bumper. It was a late model sedan. The passenger door swung open. A man jumped out and crouched behind the door.

"That son of a bitch has a gun!" Sal yelled.

Frank could see little in the intense glare of white headlights. He could see the man pointing something at them through the open window of the car. The man was resting his arms on the door. Then there were two muffled bangs, and Frank and Sal were covered in a shower of small glass fragments. Two large holes appeared in the windshield with cracks radiating from them.

Frank switched off his headlights, shoved the car in reverse, looked over his shoulder, and raced backward up the road, with only the back-up lights to guide their way. As dangerous as this was, there was no way to get around them by going forward.

There was enough light from the other car to see the road in glaring white and black shadows. He wanted to keep moving. There was no way the other car could pass and shooting forward out of the side windows was nearly impossible. Natural growth hugged the roadsides, and even if they did get off a few shots, the way the car was bucking along, it would have taken a lot of luck to hit them.

Sal had picked up his .38 chief special and was looking for an opportunity to shoot at the car.

"Not now, Sal. Wait!" Frank shouted above the thundering metallic noises the car made as it bounced and bucked from the potholes and washouts in the road. "There's a paved intersection a mile or so away. I'm going to try a one-eighty reverse turn there. When I tell you, let them have it, and try to get their plate numbers."

The Chevy's engine was whining like a high-speed turbine, and Frank hoped, even prayed, that the car would hold together long enough for them to reach the intersection. They hit a deep hole in the road. There was a sharp explosive sound, and the rear lights went out. A hideous shudder ran through the old car's body, but they were still moving in reverse. The steering wheel felt mushy and unresponsive, but he still thought he had enough control. Then the other car switched off its headlights, and for a long moment they seemed to be floating in silence near darkness, safe and serene. Until the Chevy began to tilt. It slid, turning over and over. The side doors crushed inward, and Frank was thrown against the roof several times despite his seat belt.

They rolled down the side of the hill slowly, smashing a path through small hardwood trees and fir saplings. Finally, the car came to a stop against a sturdy old-growth hickory trunk. The battered chevy lay on its roof, wheels spinning in the air and hissing out its last breath like a great dying beast.

Frank untangled himself from his seatbelt and the twisted mass of metal and crawled out of the side window. There was a strong odor of gasoline and electricity in the cold mountain air. Sal was already out on the other side, slapping the snow and mud off his jacket.

"You all right?" Frank whispered.

"Yeah, yeah, I feel okay. Christ, that was some driving until those creeps turned their lights off."

Spotlights appeared on the invisible road above them. Intense white rays traveled over their heads toward the stars.

"Let's go," Frank said. "I think I know where we are. If I'm right, there's a small lake just over there." He pointed down the hill. "We have to get to the other side of that lake."

They felt their way down the hillside, occasionally sliding on loose snow or the slick surface of a hidden rock. There were plenty of trees, so they always had good cover and a solid hand-hold before taking a step. When they reached the edge of the lake, Frank pushed through the tall, brittle reeds and tested the ice with his foot.

"I think the ice is thick enough. It's only about a quarter mile across, but going around will take us over two miles, and they are bound to catch us."

"Won't they be able to track us? I mean, we're gonna leave tracks in the snow out there." Sal motioned toward the black void of the lake.

Frank reached down to feel the ice beneath his feet. "I don't think so. The rain has turned the snow into rough ice. But it's a chance we've got to take."

All the lights overhead turned off except for one, a very powerful searchlight that pointed down the hill and swept through the trees like a white sword.

"That does it," Sal said. "Let's go."

Frank started across the ice, moving as fast as he could on flat feet to get every ounce of traction and present as much surface area on the ice as his shoes allowed. The light darted mercilessly behind them, searching frantically, coming closer with each sweep.

Sal struggled on the ice. He was trying to run too hard and slipping too much, and he was dropping behind. Frank could make out the dark line of the shore ahead. Then, with a slight crack, Frank felt the ice beneath him begin to give way. He lunged and landed belly first on harder ice, skidding and spinning slowly, as if in a dream of falling. When he finally slid to a stop, he scrambled to his feet, glanced around for Sal, but did not see him. He started again for the shoreline.

Then he was diving through thick reeds and dropping down to flatten himself in their muddy, icy roots. He lay quiet, moving only his eyes, following the searchlight as it jerked back and forth. He listened for Sal. He should be somewhere nearby, but there was nothing—no sound, no movement except for the silent, deadly finger of light, relentlessly searching.

The light stopped, moved back, and caught Sal on the end of its glowing shaft. He was up to his chest in a pool of water, desperately trying to crawl back onto the ice. He seemed unaware that the light had found him.

There was a quick tap-tap-tap-tap-tap from the hillside, like someone tapping on window glass with a pencil point. Sal was instantly surrounded by small explosions of ice and water. He stiffened for a moment, then slipped, slowly, off the shelf of ice and into the pool of water. The light held the pool until the ripples stopped, then turned off. Frank could hear the movements of more than one man making their way back up the hill to the road. Falling chunks of ice and rock clattered on the frozen lake's surface.

Frank lay shivering in the mud until he was sure they had not taken the road around to this side of the lake. Perhaps they thought he was the first to go through the ice and never made it out. Or maybe they were only after Sal, and either arrogantly or foolishly ignored him. Whatever the reason, he couldn't take unnecessary chances now, and even though they probably did not know where his cabin was, he decided not to risk going there. Slowly, stiffly, he got to his knees and gently pushed the reeds aside to look at the lake. Nothing stirred, and it was as black and empty as before. The hole in the ice would be frozen over tomorrow, and Sal would be sealed there until spring, with his pockets stuffed full of money, legal papers, and a gun.

Frank's hands had numbed to the point where he could not feel the mud that he scraped off his clothes, and his feet were like solid blocks of wood. He started up the hill, careful to place his feet on firm ground. The reeds had given way to thick forest.

He hooked his arms around tree trunks to pull himself along. By the time he reached the dirt road, he was beginning to get some feeling back in his extremities.

When he was a young and hungry charter pilot, he remembered waiting outside the locked operator's office in twenty-degree weather for his passenger to return. He couldn't waste precious aviation fuel just to stay warm, so he'd spent most of the night sprinting up and down the taxiway, working up body steam that would soon be drawn away by the cold. Cold was like death. It was always trying to get at you, seeping in under doors, through windows, always drawing life-giving heat from your body.

Frank reached the road after one last struggle with the mud and snow. He knew there was a house several miles down the road. He didn't know the people who lived there, but that didn't matter now. All he could think about was the cold that threatened to kill him.

He ran down the road, flapping his arms like a wingless bird in an absurd attempt at flight. The movement warmed him a little but running in this kind of total darkness was impossible. The road was muddy and invisible beneath him. Trotting worked a little better, and nothing interfered with flapping his arms. He pumped up a little more body heat and concentrated on his arms to forget about the cold.

How far was the farmhouse? He had always judged distance from his cabin. He was not completely sure of his position on the road. He kept trotting, planting his feet firmly in the soft surface of the road, occasionally stumbling but never quite falling.

The glow of car headlights appeared behind him. They were hidden by a curve and had not caught him in their direct beams yet. He reached the edge of the road in three long strides, grabbed a small fir tree at the top like he would an adversary by the hair, and jumped off the road. The tree bent over nearly ninety degrees and checked his momentum. He released it, and it snapped back upright. It would take more than Frank to break off its maturity.

He worked his way down several feet below road level,

digging the toes of his shoes into the ground for support. The car approached slowly, the tires grinding overhead. He hoped they were just locals who knew the condition of the road, maybe even the people who lived in the house that he was looking for. But Frank wasn't thinking of that by the time the car passed.

He was thinking of Baja, California, in July. He could almost feel the blistering sun, smell the dry desert air. He could see the blue Pacific glittering all the way to the horizon and hear the refreshing sound of the Pacific waves crashing on the rocky shore.

His memory of Baja was so clear that he believed for a few quick moments that he had awakened there. Maybe he had passed out and the people in the car had found him, and somehow his comatose body had been sent to California for treatment at an elegant hacienda, letting the sun and Pacific revive him.

He abruptly regained consciousness, gazed around, and wiped the snow away from his mouth. It tasted like foul ice water. The wind had started to pick up, and it had a Canadian bite to it. Tomorrow everything would be frozen solid. He pushed himself up from the ground, forced several deep swallows of cold air into his lungs, and struggled back up to the road.

CHAPTER 12

Frank held the large white sign, at the entrance to a driveway, with both hands to keep it steady in the biting wind. There was just enough starlight to see it. It read, "Corey's Christmas Tree Farm, est. 1990." He walked down the long drive, bordered on both sides by rows of pointed, ice-covered fir trees that were about his height.

When he reached the point where the driveway divided into a circle in front of the house, a curtain of floodlights turned on, and the house disappeared behind the intense light. Frank covered his face with his arm, but the light seemed to penetrate it and stab to the back of his head.

A loud male voice came out of the wall of light. "Who are you and what do you want?"

"I've had an accident. I missed the turn and ran my car off the road. I would like to call someone to pick me up."

A dog was barking nearby. After a long minute, the lights switched off. Frank lowered his arm slowly. The silhouette of a large man and a dog stood in the open doorway.

"Come in," the man said, backing into the house and pulling the dog with him.

The place looked so warm and snug inside that Frank hesitated at the door and wiped his shoes on the door mat. Once inside, the man reached around behind Frank and closed the door.

"You say your car ran off of the road?"

"Yes."

Frank couldn't believe what he saw. The man looked like Santa in one of those old Coca-Cola Christmas ads, with his sleigh in the background as he enjoyed a large Coke. He was even wearing a red-and-black-checkered wool shirt, dark wool pants, and hunting boots. His cheeks were round and pink like Santa's, his hair was thick and white, his eyes blue and merry, and he grew Christmas trees.

"You're Mr. Corey?"

"Yes, Jim Corey. Corey for short. And this is Chance." Corey tugged at the leash of his Doberman Pinscher.

The dog glared at Frank with a primitive fury in its eyes. It seemed on the verge of a killing frenzy. Frank backed away a few steps.

Corey laughed. "Don't worry. He wouldn't hurt you. He's all bluff. Aren't you, baby?" He bent down, kissed the dog behind the ear, and vigorously scratched his head. Still, the dog stared at Frank, saliva dripping from its mouth.

"Just a pussy cat," Corey cooed in the dog's ear. He gave the dog a slap on the shoulder and stood up. "The phone is over there."

Frank turned in the direction Corey indicated. It was a wall phone in the kitchen. Feeling like he was going to collapse, he pulled one of the bar stools over and sat on it. He dialed the Major's number and waited.

When he first met her, the Major had been a young Air Force nurse assigned to the Pentagon. He was still on staff at the NTSB and had been divorced from his wife for a week. That night at the bar, he drank a little too much and talked a little too loudly with the woman on the next barstool. The Major, as he deliberately called her, sensed the greater problem, and with nurse-like interest, she'd driven him home and saw him safely into bed where she resisted his drunken advances. However, she did leave her business card on his living room table. The next day, after he had succeeded in quieting the thunder in his head and had summoned up enough courage to face his guilt, he called her number on the card. He'd tried his most apologetic voice, and she assured him that he had been a near perfect gentleman and that she would be happy to have dinner with him as soon as he felt sufficiently recovered.

Frank was going to let the phone ring forever until somebody out there picked it up.

"Hello?" It was the Major's voice, sounding rushed and breathless.

"Major, it's Frank. I don't have time to explain. Could you come and get me? I've had an accident."

"Where are you?" She sounded concerned.

"Hang on a minute." Frank looked at Corey. "Correct me if I make a mistake, okay?"

Corey nodded.

"Take 50 west from DC to Timber Ridge Road, then take the first left. That'll be 52, about six miles down that road."

"He'll see the sign. I'll have the lights on," Corey added.

Frank repeated it into the phone.

"Isn't that near your place?" she asked.

"Yes."

The Major hesitated. "You can't tell me about it now, can you?"

"No."

Another hesitation.

"Make it as fast as you can. I don't want to inconvenience Mr. Corey any longer than I have already."

"Okay, love. But you owe me, and you're going to pay up this time."

"Sure, whatever you say."

Frank could hear her laughing as she hung up. The Major was tough, but not invincible. That was one of the things he liked about her. Like him, she had been through marriage once and wasn't anxious to repeat it. She had learned that it was truly possible to make love, even feel love, without the compulsion of marriage.

"I'm not ready to go through that whole possessive, master-slave thing again," she had clarified. That was the only note of finality she had ever used with him.

He had never been comfortable with the concept of finality. The thought of something coming to an absolute, irrevocable end was always disturbing. He wanted things to go on and on. Ironically, "finality" was the plain and simple truth of his business and, it seemed, of the entire universe, but he never grew to like it. He called the major occasionally for a dinner date, for a skiing weekend, or when he just wanted to be with her.

"Why don't you get out of those clothes," Corey said, interrupting his thoughts. "It'll be a while yet before your friend gets here. Take a nice, hot bath. I'll throw your things in the dryer. Here, take this." He handed Frank a thick, flannel bathrobe.

Frank lay in the bath water, feeling the restorative heat oozing into his body. The hot water was painful at first, but after a few minutes it became warm and caressing.

He thought of Sal under the ice, his body probably lying on the hard bottom of the lake. He wanted to ask him if it was worth it, but he knew the answer to that. Life is all one really has and if one loses it, then there is nothing left. Frank wondered if Sal had considered that in those last vital seconds of his life.

He stayed in the bath for over thirty minutes, until the water felt lukewarm, and the tips of his fingers were wrinkled like dried fruit.

He toweled dry in the flow of warm air blasting from the heating vent, slipped into the oversized robe, brushed his hair into some uniform arrangement, and stepped into Corey's large living room.

"Here, see how you like this," Corey said, thrusting a glass of apple brandy in front of him. "Made it myself from my orchard." He smiled and put his finger to his mouth. "But don't tell anyone."

Frank tasted the brandy. It burned delightfully down to his center, then defused in warming rays throughout his body. "This is delicious," he said, holding the snifter up to his eyes, "and it's very kind of you to help me out like this."

Corey smiled. His cheeks glowed red as he poured himself a half snifter of the apple brandy. "You could have frozen to death out there."

The Doberman settled down comfortably beside him. It was still attached to Corey by a sturdy chain.

"What can I say but thanks?"

"Have a seat, please."

Corey seemed a little embarrassed. "Your things are in the dryer. They should be ready in a few minutes."

Frank sat in one of the chairs closest to the fireplace. Corey lit his pipe, and Frank noticed his eyes glancing at him above the flame of the lighter. Corey took a long drag from the pipe and waved the smoke away with his hand.

"Now." There was that hard tone of finality again. "Why don't you tell me the real reason you're here."

"I didn't lie to you, Mr. Corey. My car did run off the road."

"And did it go all the way into the lake? There is lake mud inside your shoes and all over your clothes, and . . . there's this." Corey held up Frank's business card and read it out loud: "Franklin C. Adams, Accident Investigative Consultant."

His eyes had lost their merriment. They were more like ovals of blue-cut glass. Frank began to feel very vulnerable. He couldn't charge into the deep freeze outside without his clothes, and even if he could, there was always Chance, the Doberman who continued to cast hungry glances his way.

"Believe me, Mr. Corey, it's best if you don't know. I'm not sure myself what the extent of the situation is."

Corey nodded. "Well, of course, that's your business. I certainly will not insist. I only thought that maybe I could be of some help."

"Some help?" Frank repeated.

"Yes. I spent thirty years in the Washington Metropolitan Police Force. I retired about five years ago to become a gentleman farmer. But to tell you the truth, I miss the work, the city, all of it."

Corey lowered his pipe and looked beyond Frank. "Most of all, I miss the people—the men and women I worked with, even the whores, pimps, and petty thieves. Funny, isn't it? The last ten years I was on the force, all I could think about was buying a place like this and finding some peace and quiet. The problem with peace and quiet is that is all there is. Nothing but peace and quiet.

"Even my wife can't take it. She decided to visit the grandkids in Florida this winter. She called the other day and said that she had to stay longer, something about the kids being sick, her help being needed, that sort of thing. The truth is, I think she is sick and tired of the cold, the never-ending wind, all those damned trees, and staring across the room at me."

Corey leveled his eyes at Frank. His face demanded the truth. "I know you're working on something around here, and somebody gave you a bad tumble. I can always tell when a man is on the run."

Despite the luxurious bathrobe, Frank felt oddly naked. He wanted his clothes back, and he didn't want to be thrown out, not before the major arrived. He decided to tell Corey something to satisfy his doubts, but not everything.

"You're right," Frank hesitated, then continued, "my . . . um, partner and I were following a man up here. His wife hired me to get some hard evidence to prove he was cheating on her. We tailed him and his girlfriend here, and they ambushed us on one of your narrow roads. I tried to get the car turned around, but we were taking hits, and the road being what it was, we rolled over the side. We tried to make it across the lake back there. I'm really lucky, and I can promise you one thing: I'm never going to take another divorce case again."

"Where's your partner? I believe you said you had a partner?"

Frank didn't think it would be a good idea to tell Mr. Corey that Sal was somewhere at the bottom of the lake. He had already lied to him about his reason for being there, and one more strategic lie wouldn't do a lot of damage.

"We got seperated in the dark. I don't know where he is."

"You see," Corey said, "I'm having trouble understanding why an accident investigative consultant would be working a divorce case."

"Sometimes you need the money," Frank said.

"Hmmmm," Corey nodded, "that makes you a dangerous man. Now he's got to make sure you don't get to the police."

Corey hesitated. Frank could almost see thoughts flashing behind his eyes.

"But his motive? It's a bit too obvious, isn't it? I mean, why—"

Frank interrupted, "Men in his situation aren't usually very rational, are they, Mr. Corey?"

Corey smiled. Frank suspected Corey sensed an indiscretion. Years of police work had taught him to recognize a cover story when he heard one, but he let it pass.

Corey placed his pipe in its holder next to the ashtray. "I'm sure your things are dry by now," he said with a smile, and ambled away, leading Chance to the utility room. The dog was like a good-natured polar bear with a devoted seal as a pet.

Frank dressed hurriedly, grateful for the decadently warm clothes. The major would be arriving at any moment, and he wanted to get back to DC as soon as possible.

Corey returned with two more brandies as Frank was fastening the last button on his shirt.

"How about one more brandy before you go?"

At that moment, the dog stood up and tensed its entire body.

"Chance seems to hear your friend coming down the drive."

Frank took the brandy and thanked Corey in a formal way for his help and kindness.

"Here's my phone number," Corey said, stuffing a folded piece of white paper into Frank's shirt pocket. "If you ever need help, even if it's just for muscle, give me a call."

Corey held Chance tightly as the major approached the front door. "Come in, come in!"

A tall slender woman dressed in a tailored mid-length winter coat breezed through the door. Her plaid cashmere scarf made famous by Burberry's of London was wrapped snuggly around her head.

She smiled, stamped her feet at the grate, and exclaimed, "Mr. Corey, I presume? You have a magical place here. I love it!"

Frank stepped forward, saying, "Mr. Corey, I'd like to

introduce you to my very good friend whom I lovingly call 'The major.'"

Corey looked surprised. It was clear he had expected The Major to be a man. "You must be a friend to come way out here in the middle of the night on a rescue mission," he said with a smile.

"Well, Frank doesn't ask for help very often, but I know him well enough to know he would never ask me for help frivolously."

She turned and looked at Frank. "Right, Frank?"

"Uh, absolutely!" Frank said with some embarrassment.

"I was telling Mr. Adams," Corey continued. "That I would love to be called upon to help out sometime if he ever needs a strong arm or some muscle. I was in the DC police force for a long time, and I know how investigations work. Purely pro bono of course. I'd just like to keep my hand in it occasionally." He paused. "Would you like a glass of homemade apple brandy to warm your innards?"

"That's very kind of you, Mr. Corey, but we have to get back to DC," the major said.

"If you must go, you must go. Here's to your success."

Corey held up his glass of brandy in a toast, and Frank mirrored the gesture.

On the drive into DC, the major waited for Frank to explain what he was doing at Corey's farm without transportation. Frank found himself being open and honest, despite how hard he tried not to be. She had that effect on him. She seemed to have that effect on others as well.

"Somebody out there may be after me, but . . ." Frank hesitated. "Maybe not. Maybe all they wanted was Sal, but I doubt it. They probably assumed that Sal told me everything, which he did not."

"But they don't know that." the Major injected.

"It could be dangerous. I'll hole up in a motel for a few days. Vickie can get word to me when the coast is clear."

"Nonsense, I won't hear of it. How often do we get to see each other? And besides, if there's any excitement involved, I want to be in on it. You can't imagine how dull the nursing profession has become these days, especially in my single state."

She had recently broken off a relationship with a first-year resident at George Washington Hospital.

"I didn't think a ten-year difference in our ages would matter, but what do you think happened? The whole affair degenerated into some murky Freudian thing. It got to where, when it was over in bed, I was patting him on his little head and calling him a good boy. He was a very pretty boy, too, but what I wouldn't have given for a grown man."

She sighed, a bit too theatrically, Frank thought.

"All the best men are either disgustingly faithful or critically wounded," she said, glancing at Frank with a wry smile. "Like you, darling."

Frank started to speak, but she held up her hand for silence.

"Please, don't hurt my feelings. I insist, and that's all there is to it . . . Oh, don't look so worried. I won't crawl into bed with you. At least not on the first night. You need to get your strength back."

CHAPTER 13

February 21
Wednesday, morning

The major lived in a new condo in Rosslyn near the Key Bridge. "It's amazing, isn't it?" she said as she fumbled with her apartment keys. "I heard that this location used to be part of the old red-light district. A few real estate guys came in and cleaned the location out in a matter of months when the cops couldn't do it in years. And now, it's all expensive apartments and condos and a few high-end shops. Amazing, isn't it?"

She tripped the lock, opened the door slightly, and peered in.

"It's okay," she said, opening the door wider. "I always check to make sure my automatic light is on and that one of the birds didn't wiggle through the wire."

Once inside, Frank found himself facing a large walk-in narrow mesh wire cage. The major had always been full of surprises, but this was something out of the ordinary, even for her.

"I had it built for the birds a couple of weeks ago. Check the door please."

Frank pushed on the doorknob. "It's closed. Is that what you want?"

"Yes."

A small brightly colored bird flew at them and landed on the cage. It hung there by its small black talons; its bright yellow eyes fixed on them.

"Go away, Missy. Momma has nothing for you."

She tapped the cage near the bird. It fluttered away. Then she unlatched the cage. "Come quickly," she said. Frank followed her into the room, and she hurriedly relatched the cage door.

"This is not the kind of hobby I would expect you to be interested in," Frank said.

"It's cheaper than sport cars. My XKE was costing a fortune, and then one day last summer—you remember summer, don't you? I was sitting on my balcony feeling sorry for myself, and this pretty little bird landed on the next balcony. He looked at me as if to say, 'Come on, join me.' Then he flew off. Just flapped his little wings and headed out over the city. Imagine what that's like to just jump into the air and fly. I've been fascinated with birds ever since then. I mean, really into it."

"Obsessed, maybe?"

"Yes, I suppose you could say that. You know me, Frank. Once I get into something, I go whole hog."

"Yes, I know."

"Frank, I don't like your tone."

"Sorry."

Frank walked over to the south end of the balcony. The sun was just coming up. Commuters were flowing across the river into one of the most important cities in the world. From there it was decided that human beings would go into space or to the moon. From there, decisions for war or peace were made. Other decisions were more quietly made, irrevocably affecting the lives of billions of people.

It was hard to believe. Something was missing. Some vital connection—unseen, undefined—but there was something that linked the first light of the winter morning with the regular pulse of people going to the good and terrible work of that city.

The sounds of the major's apartment and the subdued flutter

of wings intruded on this deceptively peaceful scene. The major was saying something unintelligible from the kitchen.

She had turned her balcony into a glass cubicle that jutted out from the top floor of the building. Tropical plants surrounded the enclosure, all arranged to get the best sun and provide an ideal habitat for the birds. The Major could look out at the city of Washington from her glass enclosed jungle and see buildings, cars, and movement, and hear only the flutter of birds' wings and the rustle of leaves.

"How do you like it?" the major asked from over his shoulder.

"I don't know," Frank said, turning around.

"Now that's a strange answer! Everybody else thinks it's a great idea. It cost me a night out on the street to have it done, and then I had to go through all kinds of red tape. The only bad thing is that the birds crash into the glass occasionally, but they've invented some clear UV gel the birds can see. You just draw some lines on the glass with it." She pointed to the places on the glass where she intended to do this.

"I hope it works," Frank said.

"Oh, it will. The fella at the bird store said there's been a lot of research done on it, and that arranging lines in a pattern would do the job."

Frank started toward the kitchen.

"The coffee isn't ready yet. Do you want bacon and eggs?" the major shouted after him.

"Major, what time do you have to go on duty?"

"Not till noon, why?" she said, looking at him with puzzlement.

"I want you to do something for me."

"Sure. We agreed, remember?" the major said.

Frank lightly tapped on the kitchen countertop with his fingers. The major knew he was serious when his eyebrows furrowed.

"Vickie is probably wondering what the hell happened to

me. I want you to stop by my office. Try to look like a worried girlfriend. Tell her that I called you to say that I'm okay, but don't tell her where I am. If she insists, tell her I decided to go fishing in Cape Cod. She'll know that's code to keep quiet. I want her to find out if anybody is watching the office or my apartment. If she can confirm it, have her call me from a pay phone, if she can find one. Give her your number, but don't tell her it's yours. Make sure she knows not to call unless she is certain I'm being watched."

"Oh, you're involved in something really big. How does a mild-mannered accident investigator end up in this much trouble?"

Frank shrugged. "Sometimes accidents are arranged to kill people, which is a highly illegal and reprehensible act in most countries. You see, major, these people are good at what they do. They hire an electronics expert to arrange an airplane accident. It's the best way to take down a jet aircraft because there is almost always an intense fire that melts everything down into shiny puddles. Only in this case, the plane broke apart before it hit the ground, so not all of it burned. Our now-deceased hit man was so good, however, that not even the people at the Safety Board can say with any certainty if it was sabotage. And, let's face it, it's not a high-profile accident like one of the major airlines where three hundred people are snuffed out. It was just a small private business jet, no big deal. It was the right combination of everything. If the weather had been clear, the pilot could have flown the airplane with no problems. Sal knew this and simply waited for the right moment. Without his testimony, it'll just go on record as an accident of undetermined causes."

"Did he ever give testimony? Or is there any record of what he did?" The major asked.

"You know, he did mention having something up his sleeve—

some proof of some sort, if he ever needed it. But he was dead before I could get it out of him."

"So, the bad guys think he may have told you something?"

"Yes, that could be what's known as a loose end."

The major's eyes met his. "And that's you?" she asked.

"Yes, but even I'm no real threat to them. At the moment, I can only offer theory and speculation. Proof is what's needed now. And the worst part of it is that I don't know who 'them' is."

"Well, why not start with who gains the most?"

It was cut and dried to the major. It all came down to money.

"Gain what?" Frank asked with a note of urgency in his voice. "Tax-free money? Love? Hope? Freedom? Major, everybody who had anything to do with Charles Rawlson had something to gain by his death."

"And what about a conspiracy? There were three people on board. Are you sure Rawlson was the target?" The major put her finger to her cheek to emphasize the point. "Maybe the bad guys just got together and decided to eliminate their mutual problem."

Frank walked over to the glassed-in balcony and gazed across the city. "You know, I think I'll start smoking again," he said.

"No, no. Don't do that. At least not now. Find a good book. There's a bunch in the bedroom. Or go to sleep. You've been up all night. Just relax. I'm going to see Vickie in the morning, but for now, I'm going to get some much-needed sleep. I'll wake you in the morning."

The next morning, Frank was having one of the major's omelets and watched as she pulled on her heavy wool overcoat, scarf, and gloves, then took the several steps necessary and kissed Frank on the cheek. "But no girls," she said with a smile.

"No girls. I promise." Frank said as he watched her walk across the room and slip out the door.

He heard the lock engage but checked it anyway. There were

a few locks, including a good deadbolt and a useless slide and chain. Then he went around and examined the windows, the French doors on the south balcony, and even the glass ledges of the east balcony. He closed the curtains on all of them.

He was beginning to feel irrationally fearful. The events of last night replayed in his mind, appearing in quick repeating flashes. He kept seeing his car plunging down the hill, his fall on the ice, Sal being sprayed with bullets. And then the feelings overwhelmed him—the panic of escape, the probing light slicing through the night, and that total vulnerability of being exposed on the lake.

He started to feel cold again. A shiver ran through his body. He needed something hot, something to numb his mind, to black out the continuous glare of last night's events.

He went over to the major's liquor cabinet and poured a large gurgle of brandy. He thought momentarily about his self-made promise not to drink until after six in the evening, but time had not meant much in the last twelve hours. *Had it only been twelve hours?* He poured a little more brandy, walked over to the television, switched it on, settled back on the couch, and lost himself in its flickering cacophony.

He was well into a second brandy when the phone jarred him awake. A local talk show with some long-winded art critics droned in the background.

"Hello?"

It was the major. "Vickie has been very worried, but she's glad you're all right. Nothing much at the office except Mrs. Rawlson keeps calling. Vickie's going to see if anyone is hanging around your apartment."

Frank thanked her more profusely than he normally did, aware that he was slurring his words.

"You sound funny, sweetheart. Have you been into something you shouldn't have?"

Frank swore he was not guilty of any indiscretions whatsoever.

"He doth protest too much. It makes me suspicious. Well then, be careful, sweetheart. "

"Where would the English-speaking world be without Shakespeare?" Frank said.

"I've never given it a thought, love. See you later." She hung up.

Frank returned to the television and promptly fell back to sleep. The phone woke him an hour and a half later. He glanced at his watch; it was a little after noon. He reached for the phone.

"Enjoy your nap, Frank?"

"Yes," Frank said, clearing the thickness out of his throat. "Did you find out anything?"

"I think so," the major said. "It's almost impossible to tell here on K Street. It looks like everybody is watching somebody. Anyway, Vickie went by your place, and it looked like somebody was there who didn't belong. So, she checked again later and called from a coffee shop. She said she could still see him. She also said that if you wanted to come, she would hang around to keep an eye on the guy until you got there."

"Great, that's using her head. I'm on my way. See you later, and thanks."

Frank slammed the phone down, jumped into his coat, and dashed out the door.

CHAPTER 14

February, 22
Thursday, 8:30 a.m.

The Metro would be too slow, so Frank signaled urgently for a cab. One squealed to a stop in front of him. It was glossy black with a red stripe down the side. The driver was Hispanic and spoke in a strong accent. Frank did not have to tell him that he was in a hurry. The man drove as if he had personally declared war on Washington and its streets. He noticed Frank's terrified expression from the rearview mirror.

"Do not worry, senor. They will stop. It never fails, senor." The driver stopped abruptly at Frank's signal, causing them both to lurch forward. Frank reached over the seat to pay him.

"Where did you learn to drive like that, my friend?"

"In city of Boston, senor. I drive there many years before I come here. I do not like the climate there." He hesitated for a moment, looked thoughtful, then said, "I do not like the climate here either."

Frank gave him an extra five dollars. The driver smiled, baring a single brown fanglike tooth.

"You're a man of my own heart," Frank said. "I am going to live in the desert someday."

"Ahhhh, senor, when you are ready, I would be most privileged to drive you."

"What is your name?"

"It's Pedro, senor. Pedro Gonzales."

Frank patted the driver on the shoulder and stepped out of the car. He jotted down the name of the cab and phone number before it drove off. Vickie was standing in front of the cafe. She brushed at her coat nervously, then glanced at her watch. He waited until she went back into the shop before approaching her. Vickie didn't have a lot of experience with threatening situations, but she appeared to be up to the challenge. Since her first day of employment, most of his work had been safe government assignments, insurance companies, airlines, and random private jobs. All had been routine with obvious and provable causes, not the slightest hint of a crime.

Frank wanted to keep the reality from Vickie. She was erratic enough under the most stable conditions, and he didn't want to involve her in any more danger than necessary.

She looked up as he entered the cafe. In her excitement, she fumbled the thing she was holding while trying to put it back on the shelf. She smiled broadly, nervously.

"Mr. Adams, it—"

Frank made a quick motion for her to keep quiet. He walked up next to her, pretending to examine the thing she had dropped, and whispered, "Thanks, Vickie. Take the rest of the day off but call the answering service and have them take all calls."

"Mr. Adams, I . . . I—"

"Don't worry, it's going to be fine. I need to find out what that guy wants. I'll call you tonight if it's necessary."

"What . . . about tomorrow?" she asked, her brown eyes wide as a startled fawn.

"If you don't hear from me tonight, take tomorrow off too. Now, which one is he?"

"The blue Ford on the next block," Vickie said, trying not to stammer.

"Thanks," Frank said.

A flicker of desperation passed over Vickie's face. "Do you want me to call somebody, the police maybe?"

"No, I'll be okay. But see if you can track down the license plate. It's a rental, no doubt, so find out which company it is. Use your best investigative detective voice and ask them who they rented it to and what he gave for ID. They probably won't tell you but ask anyway. Leave me a message when you find out anything. I'll see you back at the office . . . whenever."

Vickie stopped at the glass entrance door of the shop, gave him a quick wave, and left. A few minutes later, Frank left the café and turned down the street. Several neighborhood kids dressed in scarves and snow jackets were throwing icy snowballs at one another.

The blue Ford was parked inconspicuously among the aging Volkswagens and Chevrolets. A heavyset man walked up the stairs of Frank's apartment building and entered. Frank thought he recognized him as Mrs. Ruiz's son in apartment I-A, but he wasn't sure. Then the man in the blue Ford stepped out of his car and hurriedly walked across the street, following the heavyset man into the building.

After a few minutes, the man in the blue Ford came back out, got into his car, and resumed his vigil.

They're not sure what I look like. They haven't had time to do the research. Probably doing it now and this guy's waiting for word.

A desperate plan began to form in Frank's mind. He had to act quickly before the man had a visitor carrying a brown envelope with photos of him. He crossed the street toward his place. From the edge of his peripheral vision, he could see the man in the car watching him. He could feel his eyes plastered all over him.

He trotted up the brick steps, and as soon as he shut the front door, he ran up to his apartment, unlocked the door, and opened it to just a crack. Then he dashed across the hall and ducked into the janitor's closet, leaving the door open enough so he had an unobstructed view of his apartment door.

In a few moments, footsteps pounded up the stairs. The man stopped outside his apartment door, glanced around the hall, reached in his coat, and pulled something to the edge of the pocket. Frank could see part of the black matt finish of a semiautomatic, which was almost completely covered by the man's hand.

The intruder examined the slightly opened door suspiciously, then placed his free hand on the knob and, gripping his hand on the concealed gun, pushed the door quickly open and charged in.

By the time Frank got to him, the man had the gun leveled and pointing forward, and he'd started sweeping it blindly around the apartment. Frank took a deep breath and put all his kinetic energy into one well-placed kick to the center of the man's back. The man lunged further into the apartment, arms and legs spread out, head thrown back. The gun twisted from his hand and tumbled through space like an out-of-control satellite until it crashed against the wall, discharged a shot, and fell behind a chair. Frank landed on top of the man, and they rolled across the room, grasping and kicking for control.

The man was heavier than Frank, and he seemed to have superhuman strength. He threw Frank off as easily as he would brush a fly off his lapel, then scrambled to his feet, looking around frantically for the gun. Frank was much slower to recover. He had only managed to stand up when the man charged at him again, teeth bared, with arms and hands extended toward his throat.

Frank waited a few seconds until the man was close enough, then rolled under him. The man fell over him, hitting his head against the wall, and fell to the floor like a bag of sticks, knocked unconscious. Frank got up quickly and examined him.

Frank needed time. He didn't know where the gun had landed. He could easily lose the next bout with this demon.

Frank raced into his workroom, found a length of cord, some rags, and a roll of duct tape. Back in the living room, he rolled the man onto his side and tied his hands and feet together, then stuffed rags into his mouth and sealed it with duct tape.

He walked over and closed the door to the hall. Owning your own place did have some advantages. No tenants were going to complain about the noise in the landlord's apartment. He searched the man's pockets but found only an airline ticket stub from London in the name of Mustafa Hafeez, several days old, but no real identification. His clothes were all new, chain-store items, probably bought with cash. He would check out the Ford for more stuff later.

He started looking for the gun; he remembered seeing it hit the wall but not where it landed. After a short search, he found it lying under his lounge chair.

The force of the shot seemed to have jammed the clip. It was a semi-automatic short barrel .22 with a silencer. He tugged at the clip and finally dislodged it. It had .22 longs with hollow points, designed to enter your body and turn your insides into hamburger. Very nasty. The favorite kill weapon of international spooks on more intimate assignments.

He had just finished pulling on his favorite wool sweater when he heard sounds of struggle from the living room. He guessed right. The man had regained consciousness and was fighting like a frenzied cat at his bonds. Frank got down on one knee next to the man's face and ripped the makeshift gag from his mouth.

"What are you doing here? Who sent you?" Frank asked.

The man's eyes were filled with a jungle ferocity. He twisted his mouth into a malicious snarl. "Do you think I'd tell you that?

Do you think I would tell you anything? You could threaten to kill me, and I would not tell you even the time of the day."

He had an accent, but Frank could not place it exactly, but guessed it was most probably Middle Eastern.

"Well, buddy, you may not tell me, but you sure as hell will tell the police."

The man snorted a short, muffled laugh. "Do you think I am afraid of you or your police? You are nothing, you and all you Americans. You are all cowards and degenerates. You will fall like wheat under the scythes of our power."

"Why were you sent to kill me?"

"I will tell you nothing. Go ahead, kill me. Or do you not even have the courage for that?"

Frank rose slowly to his feet. Perhaps it was time to call in the police. This man's blind venom suggested something far more sinister than he had imagined. Frank withdrew the gun from his pocket and slowly pointed it at the man's forehead. The hatred in the man's eyes never wavered. He was, Frank realized, prepared to die.

Frank lowered the gun and started for the phone. The man struggled wildly for a few moments, then stopped. He seemed to have calmed down; probably resigned to his fate. Frank consulted a rolodex he kept next to the phone. He found the number for the police.

His attention had been deflected for a moment when he searched the rolodex. He heard a noise—something moving quickly, like footsteps. He turned toward the noise and saw an arm raised to strike. Instinctively, he parried the blow. His reaction deflected the blow from his head, but its impact on his body knocked him to the floor. He heard the phone jingle once, then nothing. He was dazed and fighting weakly to hold onto the gun, but his attacker had all the advantages and easily wrenched the gun from his hand, then backed off.

Frank got to his feet and shook the sparks from his brain.

"You Americans, can you not do anything right? That childish piece of cord you used to tie me up. What do you think this is, some little boy's game?"

Frank didn't move. "What now?"

"I kill you, as is my duty."

"Why don't you tell me what this is all about first. What difference is it going to make?"

"It will make no difference to you, and since it will not, then you need not know. Do you not agree?" the man said.

"Except for one thing . . . there are no bullets in that gun."

The man laughed. "Such boys," he said, shaking his head like a tolerant parent.

"Why don't you check the clip."

The man smiled as he pushed the clip release lever. He seemed puzzled for an instant when nothing popped out of the grip.

"Very clever. But you forget the one in the chamber."

Frank felt a hot surge of panic rush through him. He did not move a muscle in his face. He had to bluff it. He smiled. "Now, if I had enough sense to remove the clip, would I neglect the chamber? We Americans know something about guns, you know."

"Ahhh, yes. From your gangster days, I know. But let us find out."

He leveled the gun at Frank's forehead. The end of the barrel looked big enough to crawl into. The man's black eye peered at him over the gunsight, the ruthless, mad eye of a predator.

Frank swallowed the tremor in his voice. "If you're wrong, you would look like a fool. You would have failed. You would have been beaten by an American. And I would not do you the favor of killing you, my friend. I would only remove both of your legs at the knees, and you would have to live as a beggar, in disgrace, despised in your country."

Frank waited, looking straight at the man's killer eye. The end of the gun barrel wavered slightly. The man squeezed the trigger, the hammer moving back to the cock position, then it released. There was a loud click as the hammer banged against the metal frame of the gun. The man knitted his eyebrows together in puzzlement, then pulled the trigger again—another misfire.

Frank took advantage of the moment, picked up a heavy bronze bookend from his desk, and threw it. The bookend hit the man squarely in the forehead. He dropped the gun and fell backward like a statue being pushed over.

Frank slowly walked the five or six paces over to the man. A corner of the bookend had embedded itself in the man's forehead, not deep enough to remain fixed, but deep enough to kill him. Blood ran down the man's face and onto the floor. Frank picked up the bookend and placed it back on his desk. He then went over to the gun, which was lying next to the man's body. He examined it carefully but found nothing mechanically out of place. He aimed it at the man's chest and squeezed the trigger. The gun fired, and Frank leaped back, dropping the gun.

He assumed the gun had been damaged when it hit the wall, but he didn't know to what extent. He had not expected it to go off, but he was curious to see if it would fire or if it was permanently damaged. He stood there looking down at the body and became overwhelmed by the thought that the lone bullet could have killed him. He stood very still as his thoughts engulfed him. He felt no pity for the man, only relief that he was still alive.

Frank knelt beside the man and turned him over. He seemed to deflate into a crumpled wadding of clothes. The 22-caliber bullet had made a small entry wound near his heart, but there was no exit wound. The bullet had done what it had been designed to do. It had entered the man's chest and spread out like an umbrella. It then penetrated his heart, leaving behind a gray, bloody pulp in its track. There was little blood because the man was already dead and the entry wound was small with no exit wound.

Frank stood up and took a step back. The man's face was as blank as an empty wall. His eyes had lost their flame and fury and now looked like dull black stones.

He really was dead, killed in Frank's apartment. The only living being that Frank had ever killed was a deer while on his only hunting trip. The deer ran from him, trying hopelessly to flee death. Even though it was mortally wounded, it ran. Then when it dropped Frank ran to it and reached it while it was still alive. The deer lay on the wet ground breathing slowly, blood and saliva running slowly from its mouth and nose. It looked at Frank, not accusingly, but as if to ask why.

Frank watched as the ebbing light and life darkened the deer's eyes, and it lay still as earth. Frank swore to himself then that he would never kill again. It would have been different if the deer had been attacking him, but the deer was running away in terror, running for its life.

Now the man lay on the floor looking much like that slain deer, but, unlike the deer, Frank could feel no pity for him. The man was himself a killer and had tried to kill Frank. Frank looked at his watch, then at the window. There was still an hour of daylight left, and the sky was filled with a dull yellow winter light, like a single small candle in an empty room.

Frank could not wait for darkness. Too much could happen before then. He had to get rid of the man's body immediately. He thought about calling the police, and if this man had been a common burglar, he would have. But now he was involved too deeply, and how deep, he still did not understand. He simply did not trust police methods; they had a bulldozer mentality and usually took the most obvious path.

He could not rely on them for discretion, secrecy, or help. They would go for the quick conviction every time, and the way it looked, Frank Adams would be it.

He could not find the man's car keys; they had to be in the car. Frank carefully opened his apartment door and checked the hall. It was clear. Then he closed the door quietly behind him and locked it. He tiptoed down the stairs and checked the street before going out. Some children were kicking a soccer ball in the street and laughing as they slipped on ice.

He walked casually over to the blue Ford. The children didn't seem to notice him. He got in on the driver's side. The man was certainly not used to driving around DC. He had left the keys in the ignition, probably not expecting to stay long. The name and number of the rental company were stamped in clear plastic on the key chain. He started the car, checked for traffic, pulled out into the street, and drove halfway around the block to the alleyway behind his building.

Except for the growing darkness, nothing had changed in his apartment. He wistfully imagined that his attacker had somehow resurrected and would say it was all an unpleasant mistake, tip his hat, and leave. But nothing had moved. Time seemed to have frozen. The dead man was as still as a piece of furniture. Nothing in the whole inventory of human knowledge could get him to stand up and walk out on his own.

Frank would have to try the "drunk friend" act, but first he needed to contain the blood oozing from the man's head and hide the blood stain on his clothes and cover the man's face.

He found a faded trench coat that he hadn't worn in years, slid the man's arms into it, and buttoned it down the front. He used rags to wash the blood from his head and face. Then he retrieved the half-empty bottle of Glenlivet from his liquor cabinet and poured some of it on the man's clothes.

Frank took the gun to his small workroom and removed all identifying numbers with his electric grinder. After wiping it down and reinserting the clip, he scrubbed his hands and forearms thoroughly, put on his gloves, and picked the gun up by its muzzle and put it into the trench coat pocket.

Frank wriggled into his brown overcoat, thankful that it was just an ordinary, bland garment, and put on an old New York Yankees baseball cap, pulling it tightly over his head. He found a wide-brimmed fedora he had worn in a local theatrical production and pulled it rakishly over the man's head. He counted on the CCTV cameras being mounted above the window level of the car and angled down. In that case, the wide brim would cover the man's face. He then tried closing the man's eyes, but one kept popping open, as if mocking his efforts. He covered the man's eyes with a pair of old sunglasses. No one would notice. Washington was full of men wearing sunglasses year-round, day and night. He draped the man's arm around his neck and pulled him up. It was like hauling a 180-pound bag of sand by a large rope. He held the bottle of scotch and the man's arm with one hand and gripped his waist with the other.

Gradually, Frank started for the back door, stumbling under the weight. He shifted the man's position slightly so that his legs kicked and slid around like an oversized puppet.

Frank gave a silent moment of thanks to the previous owner for installing a fire escape at the back of the building. The rails could easily support the two of them. Frank slowly slid the corpse along the iron rail against the building. Halfway down, he noticed one of the older tenants in the next building staring down at him from her top floor window. Her arms were crossed in front of her, and she looked disgusted. Frank held the bottle of scotch up and waved to her with it. He hoped she would get the wrong idea.

After a lot of grunting and effort, he managed to get the man into the front passenger seat of the car. He decided to drive across town and leave the car in the Kennedy Center parking garage. It was the one place he knew that a rented car would be ignored for a while, and there was no attendant at the entrance gate.

He was relieved there wasn't a line at the entrance gate and was able to approach without stopping. Frank pulled the brim of his baseball cap down to his eyes to shield his face from the CCTV camera. He approached the ticket machine. The machine buzzed and clicked, then spit out a ticket. He pulled the ticket out against the slight resistance of the machine, and the wooden arm in front of him rose quickly. He drove under it, wondering ludicrously if it ever came down on anyone.

The garage was about half-full. Apparently, the performance that everyone had come to see was well underway because no one was around. He drove into a space between two large SUVs, looked around, then got out of the car. He went around to the other side of the car, opened the door just enough to squeeze in, and pushed the man behind the wheel. He pulled and tugged on the trench coat until he finally got it off the man's body. He then arranged the man's clothes to look as though he had been driving. He lowered the man's arm onto the seat and placed the gun in his right hand.

Frank wiped down any surface he may have touched. His attention was drawn to the scotch bottle on the car floor, and he grabbed it by the neck and stuffed it into his jacket pocket. No matter how he tried to hide it, his jacket bulged conspicuously, and it would be sure to draw attention. He wiped it clean with his handkerchief, spilled a little of the scotch on the floor, and dropped the bottle there. Mustafa Hafeez—or whatever his real name was—would be, at first examination, just another suicide in a dark and empty place, drinking some courage before pulling the trigger.

He shut the car door wiping it clean with his handkerchief and glanced around the garage at the concrete ceiling and the heavy, concrete pillars supporting it. The grayish halls and dim lighting seemed to be an acceptable tomb for his would-be assassin, a secular, man-made catacomb for the thugs of DC. He took a few deep breaths and enjoyed the sense of relief that came with it. He turned and started up the two flights of stairs to the street floor and exited through the main hall. It made him think of a glass cathedral. The performance underway was *Richard II*.

CHAPTER 15

February 22
Thursday, 10:30 a.m.

Frank called his office phone to check his voicemail. There was a message from Vickie, and her voice sounded tense.

"I'm sorry I've taken so long. But anyway, the guy's name is Mustafa Hafeez. He's listed with Customs and Immigration as a sales rep for an investment company, but when I called, all I got was a recording saying that someone would get back to me. The company's located in London. I have a friend who works at the British Embassy, and she knows a lot of people there. You want me to have her ask around? Anyway, I hope you're okay. Let me know if you want me to call the police. They could run a fast check on this man, find out just what his mission is—"

He quickly punched in Vickie's mobile phone number. It went straight to voicemail. He left her a message.

"Absolutely not," Frank said. "Do not call the police. I repeat, do not call the police. I will let you know when that will be necessary." He hesitated a few moments to stress the importance of it. "Thanks for looking into Mustafa Hafeez. See what your friend at the British Embassy can find out about this investment company. And continue looking into Amertek Electronics. Write out a report and leave it in the office safe. Keep up the good work." He hung up the phone.

The major was standing in the doorway to the kitchen. "Why

don't you let her bring in the police? This whole thing has gotten pretty nasty," she said with one hand resting on her hip.

"Listen, if the police find out I was connected with Hafeez's death, the first thing they'd do is arrest me for murder. Then they'd find traces of his blood on my carpet, his prints all over my living room, and pieces of his hair and God knows what else. Are they going to believe me when I tell them that this professional assassin 'sales rep' just made the dumbest mistake anyone can make with a handgun? No. I can hear them laughing all the way to the prison nut ward. I have to find out more about it. This guy was no ordinary hit man. He was dedicated far beyond the call of money. He was more like some ideological fanatic on a divine mission."

"A terrorist, maybe?"

Frank shook his head. "A fanatic, yes, but not that kind of fanatic. He was too clean, too well fed. The papers might make a terrorist story out of it, but somehow, I don't see it."

"You know, I haven't seen a thing about it in the paper."

"I don't think enough time has passed. The clean-up crew is probably just finding him now. But you're right. They're certainly not going to let it get out that a man was found shot to death in the parking garage of the Kennedy Center, do you?"

"I have to admit it, Frank. That was smart."

"It was desperation and the intense desire to survive, at least long enough to find out who's behind all of this. It won't take the police long to figure out that it wasn't a suicide, but it may buy me enough time to get to the bottom of this. Wow!" Frank said, looking at his watch. "I've got to run. I have a very important date with a very classy lady."

"What?" the major said. "You mean the rich, youngish, widowed client? Tell me, is it those eyes, the blonde hair, the seductive way she moves her lips?" She moved closer to his face and didn't bother to conceal the acrimony in her voice.

"She isn't blonde. She has chestnut-brown hair."

"How elegant. And I suppose she had it done up in a chignon, huh?"

"No, and I love it when you're jealous."

"Of course, I'm jealous of anyone who doesn't have to work."

"Now, major, don't get catty. Mrs. Rawlson can't help that she has everything: money, intelligence, eternal youth, and stunning beauty. It's not her fault. Besides, she's out of my league. Jet-set material. I'm just a humble proletarian, hustling for a buck, and you're still the fairest in the land, my general."

"Frank, I've always wanted to tell you something. I'm not a major, a captain, or even a general. I've been out of the service for years. I'm a surgical nurse, and my name is Ann Harris and . . . never mind." Then she said with sudden disinterest, "When will you be back?"

"If things go the way I want them to, it'll be very early tomorrow morning." He smiled. "Oh, I forgot. I need to borrow your car."

"Get outta here," she said, tossing the keys his way.

Mrs. Rawlson sounded curious over the phone and agreed to meet Frank at Lord Byron's. "But" she warned, "I don't have much time."

Frank ordered a beer and sat in one of the booths where, as usual, he could see the door. He always liked Lord Byron's. It was deceptive from the outside, just a door and a small sign. In the summer, a few outside tables crowded the narrow front, but inside it seemed to go on forever, through what appeared to be adjoining caves and tunnels and old cellars. It was rumored that the caves had been an escape route for slaves fleeing north during the Civil War. The owner of Lord Byron's claimed to have found some rusted weapons and a skeleton still wearing the tattered remains of his Union Army uniform.

Everything in Lord Byron's glittered with reflected light. The tables glowed with thick, clear varnish. Metal and glass sparkled with gold and silver and polished brass.

The clientele seemed genuine. Sunday Brunch was a popular draw for special occasions or business meals for out-of-town clients. The workaday business crowd would gather here after working hours for drinks and quiet talk. No local musical group rented the air with discordant sounds. No jukebox thumped out the latest rock hit. No big-screen TVs silently flashing sports games on every wall.

Frank ordered another beer and saw Mrs. Rawlson standing inside the doorway, seemingly hesitant to enter. He waved. She spotted him at once and started toward his table. Frank motioned for her to sit down. She hesitated, examined the seat in one quick sweep of her eyes, and joined him.

"Would you like something?" Frank asked.

She met his eyes straight on. "No, no thank you." She was impatient and ill at ease. "Well?" she demanded.

"Your husband was murdered."

Frank waited for this to sink in. Mrs. Rawlson showed no reaction.

"The man who did it is now at the bottom of a mountain lake in Virginia, and I almost joined him there. He was also murdered, and I think it was the same people who paid him to kill your husband."

"Do you know who they are?" Mrs. Rawlson asked as calmly as she would have asked for a dinner menu.

"No, but—"

"Well, that's it then," she interrupted. "My husband was murdered."

"Yes, but I can't prove it."

"I see," she said stiffly. "Then it's a matter for the police."

"Yes, but not immediately."

She looked puzzled.

"Somebody tried to kill me too. They seem to be after me now, and I want to know why. I need your help."

She remained silent; her eyebrows arched. "Maybe they think you can prove their guilt?" she said dispassionately.

"They do. But as of right now, I can't prove anything. I need evidence. I'm confident I can get answers from your father's private papers. Can you get me access?"

She paled, and her lips trembled slightly. "Absolutely not." Her eyes narrowed. "Are you saying that my father is involved in Charlie's death? That's the most disgusting thing I've ever heard. You have the murderer, or at least you had him. He apparently confessed to you. That's enough, isn't it?"

"He was only paid to do the job, but he didn't know who was really paying him. The guy had been an Amertek employee and knew the inner workings of the company. Your husband's death was ordered by someone or some group."

"Why? I knew my husband had had a few indiscretions, but from what I've learned, he never forced himself on anybody. They were all too willing. Aggressive, ambitious men are like that. It's expected."

"Did you know your husband was bisexual?"

Her mouth dropped open for a moment and her eyes widened. "That's absurd," she whispered. "I would know. I, I would have known," she corrected. "It's ridiculous, a vicious rumor started by his enemies. That's all it is."

"So why did you want me to investigate the accident?"

"To find out if it was an accident, of course. If some stupid, jealous person is responsible for this, I want him brought to justice."

"And if it isn't a jealous husband? If it goes in another direction?"

"I'm not going to listen to any more of this nonsense!" She slammed her purse on the table and took out a checkbook and pen. "What do I owe you, Mr. Adams?"

"My secretary will send you a bill."

"Well, please address it to my accountant," she said. "You'll save us both time." She started to leave the table.

"Mrs. Rawlson, I'm going to have to go to the police once you no longer require my services. Your father will be one of the first people they investigate, and police methods tend to be rather democratic and complete. You see, everyone had a reason to kill your husband, even you."

She lowered herself back into the seat. "So why do you think my father had anything to do with it?"

"I'm not certain he did, but your husband was next in line, and as you said, he was aggressive and ambitious. Maybe someone wanted to change the line of succession. Or maybe kings do not give up their thrones so easily."

"My father, you mean?"

"Yes."

She looked to one side and chewed on the corner of her mouth. "Well, I know it wasn't my father. He's been ill and was grooming Charlie for the job, but there are quite a few 'ambitious' men in the company."

She looked straight at Frank. "All right, I'll re-engage your services to find out who actually murdered Charlie, or at least to find evidence that would clear Daddy and me. I'll take you out to the house." She sighed. "Good God, I hope my father never finds out. He'd never forgive me."

CHAPTER 16

February 22
Thursday, 4:25 p.m.

I t was nearly dark by the time they arrived in Middleburg. At Frank's suggestion, Mrs. Rawlson entered the Russell estate from the back service entrance. It was a long, winding gravel road that curved through dark pools of shadow beneath hanging trees. The house appeared like a dark silhouette of an abandoned chateau. It looked like a two-dimensional stage prop, outlined in a clear night sky.

"Can you park out of sight?" Frank asked.

She made an impatient sigh. "Will the carriage house do? It's empty right now. Father had his collection of antique carriages taken to a show in upstate New York."

"It's okay as long as we're not seen. Are there any house servants?" Frank asked.

"Only Harrison, a septuagenarian who's been a butler here for forty years. Even if he saw us, he wouldn't think anything of it. He's known me all my life."

Mrs. Rawlson drove slowly into the nineteenth-century carriage house. There was just enough room for the car door to open, allowing Frank to squeeze out. She whispered for him to follow and seemed surprised that she had, for an inexplicable reason, lowered her voice. In fact, she seemed very conscious of noise in general. *Maybe it was the night, the emptiness of the large estate, and the great house she had known as a child*, Frank mused.

They walked up to the service entrance by way of the wide gravel driveway, with ice crunching softly beneath their feet. Lights switched on in several windows of the house.

"Would that be Harrison, the butler?" Frank asked.

Mrs. Rawlson chuckled. "Don't worry. It's part of the security system Father installed a few years ago. There are pressure sensors located around the exterior perimeter. Anything weighing a hundred pounds or more will turn on the house lights."

"You know, I wish you had told me about this before. I don't think it's particularly smart to announce our arrival with a display of lights, do you?"

"I couldn't turn the system off if I wanted to. It's automatically controlled from the inside, and there is a backup control operated by the company who installed the thing. After all, it's only to scare away burglars, and we're not actually breaking and entering, are we?"

"Are there any more surprises?"

"Just one." She took out a small key and inserted it into a slot next to the service door. She gave it a half turn, then pressed it. The heavy metal door started rolling up into the ceiling. "This is for the alarm. Turning the key isn't good enough. The thing must be pressed in as well. Both actions turn off the system, but if you only turn the key, or try to force an opening, the alarm goes off and it sounds like World War III. A silent alarm is also triggered at two police stations."

"Has anyone ever tried to break in?"

"Unfortunately, yes. A valuable El Greco painting, some Goya etchings, and on the way out, they helped themselves to my mother's jewels and the flat silver. They knew what they were doing, all right. They got in and out without leaving a trace. Not even a chair was knocked over."

Once inside, she pressed a small white button to close the door. "The system automatically resets once the door is closed," she said with a touch of pride.

They took the service elevator to the first floor, and Frank followed her through a maze of richly decorated halls and furnished rooms to the only place he recognized in the house, Richard Russell's library turned office.

"There they are," she said, pointing to the desk.

"What? No hidden safe? Nothing like that?"

"I told you, my father has nothing to hide. Go ahead, look. The desk isn't even locked."

Frank was skeptical.

"Look at it his way. If they want it bad enough to risk getting in here, then a few puny desk drawer locks will not keep them out."

Frank started with the top drawer, carefully examining everything, even checking pencil erasers and pen interiors for hidden documents or memory chips.

There was nothing of interest until he spotted a large folder with another folder in it labeled "Lab Test Report," The report was signed by Salvatore Sassavitte. Beneath his signature, several initials were scrawled at the edge of the paper. Mrs. Rawlson said one was her husband's, but she wasn't sure of the other.

Frank flipped through the document. "This is just what I've been hoping for," he said.

"Don't move," a voice said from across the room.

It was a firm voice, smooth and controlled. Frank looked up. He could only make out the shadowy figure of a man standing across the room next to the doorway. He was holding something

. . . a gun perhaps? He reached behind him, and an overhead chandelier lit up.

"Father! I . . . I thought you were in Anguilla!"

"Helen! What?" he said. Then he glared at Frank. "And you? What are you doing here?" He motioned at Frank with his pistol. "What is this all about?"

"Oh, Daddy, please don't be angry. It's not what you think. We didn't want to alarm Harrison, and I thought you were away."

Mr. Russell rubbed his eyes with his free hand. He had clearly been sleeping and had hurriedly changed into a dressing gown.

"Well, what is it then? I can't imagine." He lowered the gun slowly, absentmindedly, as if he were no longer aware of it.

"I'll explain, Mr. Russell," Frank said. "Since we last spoke, I have discovered that your son-in-law was murdered, and I'm not sure yet why or by whom."

"And you think . . ." He turned to his daughter. Then his face flushed, and his eyes became intense blue lights. "You think I might be responsible, is that it?" He flashed his eyes at his daughter.

"Oh, Daddy, please calm down. You know you're not well." She started crying and blubbering her words. "It's not you. It's something to do with the company. We don't know. I didn't want to do this, but I just couldn't tell you what I believed about Charlie's death. I imagined it might have had something to do with one of his affairs. At least that's what I thought. You know how he was."

The old man stiffened. His prominent chin stuck out. "There were rumors, allegations—none of them ever substantiated," Mr. Russell said, clutching his chest. "And yes, there were a few men in the company who were envious of his ability, that's all."

Mrs. Rawlson sobbed into her hands. Mr. Russell laid the gun down on a side table and walked over to his daughter. He seemed lost and confused. He started to speak but swallowed it back. He looked to Frank for help.

Frank opened the Lab Test Report folder and pulled out a document. "Are these your son-in-law's initials?" he asked.

Mr. Russell looked at the paper and nodded.

"What did this mean when you got it?"

Mr. Russell's hand started to tremble slightly. "It is an itemization of defective parts in our latest logistics system. I wanted to keep it here, away from my office in Leesburg. If this information had gotten out, it would have meant financial disaster. We were in the middle of negotiating several contracts with the government, and I had a meeting with several representatives of a Chinese firm later that same week. Charles brought me the report as soon as it was put on his desk. If we had recalled those defective parts at that time, we would have risked losing the government contracts, everything. We had never had a problem like this before. All our work has been of top quality. It was unbelievable."

"It is signed by Salvatore Sassavitte. Is that who did the analysis?" asked Frank.

"Yes."

"Who commissioned the report?"

"That would be Gerald Saunders in Quality Control. I don't get along well with Saunders, so I wasn't sure what to do. Charles said he would handle it. He was sure we could wait until after the contract negotiations were completed before issuing a recall order. The parts were not scheduled for use until the first of the year, but he said he needed more authority."

"Wasn't he already the vice president?"

"Yes, but monetarily speaking, he needed a larger share of the company. I had already said I was not going to attend the meeting, so he would be handling it by himself. He wanted more pull with our investors."

"And added shares would guarantee his succession as president of the company."

"Yes," Mr. Russell went on, "we're a privately held company, but we do carry significant loans. Charles needed his investors to have confidence in him, you know. So, I gave him an option on twenty-five percent of my shares, which I had planned to turn over to him when I retired."

"Then you, your daughter, and your son-in-law would continue to hold controlling interest in the company?"

"Yes."

"And with Charles out of the picture?" Frank asked.

"I am uncertain of that now."

Frank held up the paper. "Do you recognize the other initials?"

"They're Saunders's. As head of Quality Control, he approves everything that comes out of the lab."

"Salvatore Sassavitte did the analytics. Did Saunders choose him specifically to do it?"

"That would be the standard procedure. It's also our normal procedure to route pertinent documents, especially confidential ones, to only those executives who will be directly affected by them. In this case, it was just Saunders, Charlie, and me."

"And Salvatore Sassavitte, the one who produced the report."

"Yes. And him."

"Did you know that Salvatore Sassavitte is dead?"

Mr. Russell's mouth dropped open, and he fixed his eyes on Frank, then on his daughter. "No! God no!" he exclaimed. "But how is that related to this? He was fired, wasn't he? He doesn't or didn't work for us anymore."

"Other than these original documents, are there any copies?" Frank asked.

"No. I know how that looks to you, but if it had gotten into the wrong hands and made the headlines . . . It's just the sort of thing they like to pump up into another mini-Watergate. We had no intention of deceiving anyone, Mr. Adams."

"But it turns out that the information was leaked, and word did get out anyway, isn't that right, Mr. Russell?"

"Yes, but—"

"And if it were known that you and your VPs were in possession of this knowledge while you were conducting contract negotiations, you would have been arrested for perjury. You were lying to the government, Mr. Russell, and they wouldn't have taken kindly to that. Would they?"

Mr. Russell's eyes looked panicked. "But the parts were recalled in ample time, and from what I understood from Saunders, everything is in good standing. Timing is just as important in our business as it is in anything else."

"And what happened with your contracts with the government and with the Chinese company? Were you able to retain them?"

"The government, yes. We have a long history of doing business together, and the drop in the share price was so sudden and it bounced back so quickly that I don't think they really even noticed. But Dongan Manufacturing, the Chinese company, apparently broke off all negotiations. As I mentioned, I didn't know anything about that, and Charlie's trip in January was going to be an attempt to lure them back. It turned out that it really wasn't all that necessary because Saunders had already brought in a London-based firm and was negotiating with them. Saunders has been very secretive about them, and, quite frankly, after Charlie's death, I'd rather forgotten about it."

"So, the business is fine now, despite taking a huge hit in the market. And who profited from that? Did you 'sell high and buy low,' as they say?"

"What are you talking about? I haven't bought or sold any shares at all."

"Except for the twenty-five percent of your shares that you gave to your son-in-law, Charles."

"Why yes, but he wouldn't do anything like that! Frank looked inside the folder and pulled out a sealed manilla envelope. "What's in here, Mr. Russell?"

"I don't know. I thought the only thing in that folder was the lab test report."

Frank slit open the envelope and pulled out a brokerage dossier of buy and sell trade receipts for Amertek Industries from November 15 through December 28, 1995. Mr. Russell grabbed the pages from his hands, put his glasses on, and looked at them himself.

"I swear to you, I didn't know anything about this! Yes, these signatures are Charlie's . . . and look here, those belong to Saunders! I don't know what to say! I trusted Charlie! I would have trusted him with my life!"

"Has Charles's estate been dispersed yet?" Frank asked.

"Oh goodness no, his affairs were nowhere near in order. He was a young man and was not expecting to die. No, his estate is in probate now. Why do you ask?"

"I'm willing to bet that the shares you gave back to him in October are no longer in his name, and that somewhere buried in these brokerage printouts, you'll find them in the name of Gerald Saunders. I need to get this folder to the police before Saunders gets ahold of it. There's enough evidence here to lock him away for years and probably start a murder investigation."

Mr. Russell started to tremble slightly and clutched his chest even tighter. He appeared to stumble as he made his way over to a nearby chair and eased himself onto its cushion.

"I knew Saunders was a bad apple. I knew it. If Charlie had only listened to me, none of this would have happened," he said.

"That's probably true, Mr. Russell, and your son-in-law would be alive today."

Mr. Russell stiffened and pulled his robe tighter around his body. "That was uncalled for, sir," he said with regal dignity.

"I'm sorry, Mr. Russell, but it's true. Your son-in-law was murdered, and I believe it had something to do with this report and the receipts in this folder."

"Then why wasn't it taken? My alarm system isn't foolproof. The house has been empty for more than a week—except for Harrison, of course, and he's deaf as a post."

"Maybe they didn't want to take it yet. They know it's as safe here as it would be anywhere else, except in a pile of ashes, of course," Frank said.

"So why haven't they done it?"

"That would mean exposure, and they obviously aren't ready to expose themselves. Then, Sal and I got into the act, which complicated their timeline."

An awareness began to dawn on Mr. Russell's face. "If that's true, then they have to take the risk now. And that puts Helen and me, as well as you, Mr. Adams, in considerable danger."

Frank and Mr. Russell stared at each other for a long time.

"What are we going to do?" Mr. Russell finally asked.

"Do you have a copier here?"

"No, I used to, but the darn thing was so intrusive and made such an awful noise. This is my home, Mr. Adams. I have one copier, maybe two, at the office."

The old man looked to his daughter.

"Don't you trust me, Mr. Russell?" Frank asked. "I have to know, or I leave right now."

Mr. Russell stammered something unintelligible. Mrs. Rawlson,looking at her hesitant father, nodded and said, "Yes. It's okay, Father."

Mr. Russell, with some hesitation, nodded his consent.

"Okay then. We go down to the office, make a few copies, and then I think it will be time to go to the police," Frank said.

It was a general office copier, installed obtrusively against the wall and a steady companion to the Coke machine. Mr. Russell switched it on and waited for it to warm up. He then placed the documents into the feeder tray and pressed several buttons. Seconds later, a perfect stack fell into the slot.

Frank examined it against the original. "Let's get two more like this, and I think that will do it," he said.

Mr. Russell punched the buttons several more times and two more piles fell out.

"That should do it. Go back home and we'll keep the originals here and lock them up. If anyone calls for them, be polite and accommodating, then call me immediately."

Mr. Russel put his arm around his daughter. "But what if there's violence?" he asked, looking directly at Frank.

Frank could see that they were genuinely frightened. He couldn't blame them. The threat of violence was very real and closer to them than before. Whoever wanted these reports certainly wanted more.

"Is there somewhere you can go?" Frank asked.

"To hide, you mean?" The old man was indignant at Frank's suggestion. "I've never run from anything in my life, and I'm not going to start now." He folded his arms defiantly across his chest.

"Oh, for God's sake, Daddy. Listen to him. This isn't a contretemps with the IRS. Four people have been murdered, and my husband was one of them."

Mr. Russell shook his head slowly. "No. I've spent my life

building this business, and I'm not going to just let a bunch of thugs take it away from me."

"Daddy, this is absurd. You will not accomplish anything if you're . . .." She hesitated, then added, "If you get hurt."

"I know what you are trying to say, my dear. But I don't care. I'll fight them with my bare fists if I must."

Frank smiled. "I don't think you'll have to go that far, sir. These copies will be enough to round up Saunders once they're in the hands of the police."

Mr. Russell looked relieved, if drained. "Good," he said. "I'm very tired now. Can we go home?"

"Sure," Frank consoled. He didn't mean to sound patronizing, but it came off that way.

Mrs. Rawlson drove, and Frank was in the front passenger seat while Mr. Russell rode in the back seat, quiet, dignified. He seemed like a respected general on his way to conduct a last futile battle against an overwhelming force. Frank said little also. The atmosphere of tragedy inside the car was pervasive. He tried to think of something humorous to say to lighten the mood, but everything that came to mind seemed silly or in bad taste.

Mrs. Rawlson flashed a few encouraging smiles his way. *Were those smiles signaling a sense of closure, satisfaction with my work, or maybe something as simple as my decision to call in the police?* Frank wondered. Whatever the reason, he felt that the wall between them had finally broken. He'd contact the police as soon as he got home. He would also call Joe Hunter at the NTSB and tell him about Charles Rawlson's murder. That would certainly be worth a few points in Joe's next performance evaluation.

This time, Mrs. Rawlson drove around to the front of the Russell estate, pressed a remote to open the garage door, and rolled the big car slowly in. The door closed behind them.

"Mr. Adams, you don't understand the way it is for a man in my position," Russell was saying as they walked up the few steps to the house.

As they approached the door, the entire house seemed to light up. They walked to the parlor and stopped under a large crystal chandelier.

"Amertek is a front-line electronics company. We are the ones making the breakthroughs in avionics technology today. We're pioneers, making it possible to go further and further into space technology, though we're still small compared to the industrial giants in the electronics industry. It's been a never-ending battle to remain a family-owned company. A few of us still hold the majority of shares. Helen and I and Charles owned thirty percent each, but after Charles died, his equity went to Helen. Nevertheless, we're assaulted from all sides—the big conglomerates underbidding us, and the multinationals trying to swallow us. Hardly a day goes by that I'm not approached by some representative offering to absorb us into his empire. Believe me, some of the offers are almost irresistible."

A reserve of energy sparkled in his eyes. "You see, Mr. Adams, the financial world knows what we are, and they know what our potential is. I owe it to my employees and to my investors to show them that the company's business model can work for them. I intend to keep Amertek a C corporation for as long as possible. So far, we've had no problems raising capital, and on the rare occasions that we needed a loan, the banks have been forthcoming. The costs of going public are too prohibitive, and, as I've said, I see no need to do so."

He put his arms around his daughter's shoulders. "And I owe it to her for everything she's been through. Losing her husband, her mother . . . at least she'll have all this when it's over for me," he said, gesturing with a sweeping arm.

"Oh, Daddy. I wish you wouldn't talk like that."

"We have to face facts, my dearest. I'm no longer young. Most of life is behind me now." He gave her shoulders a quick squeeze. "I had so much hope in Charles." Mr. Russell shook his head slowly. "Thank you for all you've done, Mr. Adams. I will be glad to cooperate with you and the police in any way to find everyone who is implicated in this matter."

He kissed his daughter on the cheek. It was a good-night kiss, the kind Frank remembered from his dates in high school. Then Russell walked with them to the front door.

"Daddy," Mrs. Rawlson said softly, "my car is parked in back."

The old man slapped his forehead. "You see, senility is already setting in," he said with a laugh.

He led them through the house to one of the rear entrances. "Call me. Keep me informed of the latest developments." He shook Frank's hand vigorously, kissed his daughter again, and closed the door after them.

CHAPTER 17

February 22
Thursday, 11:30 p.m.

"Y ou can let me off here," Frank said as they drove by the major's car. Mrs. Rawlson pulled over into the first open section of curb.

She turned to face him. "I'm sorry you've been exposed to so many risks. Let's get together soon, maybe celebrate. I've got a bottle of twenty-seven-year-old Redbreast Irish whiskey with your name on it. I'm so damned relieved that it's all over." Her voice was softer and more human than before.

"But it isn't all over, Mrs. Rawlson," Frank said reluctantly, knowing he might frighten her back into her frozen façade. And, wistfully, he recalled that Redbreast 27 ran around $600 a bottle.

"Not over?" she said like a puzzled child. "But you've established that my husband was murdered. That's all, isn't it? I mean, the police take it from here, right? You've done your job and done it so well . . ." She gazed at him warmly, touching his lapel.

"But we're not off the hook, Mrs. Rawlson. For one thing, the police don't know anything about anything yet. Whoever killed your husband still wants to take me out."

She moved closer to Frank and lightly touched his hand. "But you're so much smarter than they are. They're probably running around in circles right now." She leaned over and kissed him gently on the lips. "And please . . . my name is Helen."

Frank reached behind him and unlatched the car door. "I would like that," he said, feeling his face grow warm, "and I'd like to get together . . . and try that whiskey, Helen, but I really have to take care of these papers first."

"Are you sure it can't wait until morning?" she asked.

Frank edged backward toward the door.

She kissed him again. "It's been a long time since I felt like this. I bet you know all about me, but I want to know all about you."

"Suppose I stop by tomorrow night, and we'll talk about it?" he said, feeling the door's armrest dig into his back. She made a sad face, pursing her lips like a bad actress.

"I really need to get the copies of the lab report and trade receipts safely distributed to ensure you and your dad's safety," Frank said, squeezing her hand to soften the rejection. He then opened the door, which seemed to instantly clear the air inside the car.

Mrs. Rawlson dropped her sad face and said, "Tomorrow then. I should probably go back and check on Father, anyway."

Frank stepped out of the car and closed the door. Mrs. Rawlson gave him a quick wave and drove away. Frank watched the car turn down the next block and disappear along with his dreams of a tumbler of Redbreast.

He looked down the street in both directions. No one had followed them. The street was quiet and clean. It was a neighborhood of law-abiding civil servants, lawyers, and government offices. No gunshots, no screams in the night here. He chuckled quietly.

Frank checked the major's car thoroughly, using his pocket flashlight to look under the hood and body for explosives. The car was untouched. He got in, locked the door, and started the engine.

He drove to his office first, spoke to the security guard at the desk, and told him that he would be in his office for less than an hour. The guard glanced at his watch, and Frank took the elevator up to the ninth floor.

Vickie had clearly left in a hurry. Every surface was adorned with half-empty Styrofoam cups, wads of wax paper and crumpled napkins with ketchup, mustard, and lipstick stains, and hardened French fries in and around the trashcans.

He found three large manila envelopes in the office safe and placed a copy of Amertek's lab report and brokerage receipts in each. He put one copy back in the wall safe, one he would put in his safety deposit box at the Riggs bank in the morning, and the other he would deliver to the police. It was truly a police matter now, and he hoped they would not simply settle for the easy answers. There was more to it than just a simple power grab by an ambitious executive who saw the president's son-in-law screwing his way to the top.

Frank's mind wandered to Mrs. Rawlson. Why did she tolerate Charles's extramarital activities? She obviously knew about them, and she probably knew how the other company executives felt about him. Was she to be believed when she denied knowledge of her husband's bisexuality? Was it fear of a scandal, or the possibility of financial repercussions for the company? Did she not want to embarrass her father, or was she simply afraid of Charles?

She'd come to Frank because she suspected one of her father's executives had her husband murdered, but when he brought her proof that she was right, she wanted to drop it. *Maybe put a little private pressure on the murderer, maybe a little blackmail?*

Abruptly, the phone rang. The unexpected clanging startled him. He looked at his watch; it was just after midnight. He picked up the phone and pressed the Record button.

"I want to congratulate you on your fine work, Mr. Adams."

Frank recognized the voice of Saunders. "So, what can I do for you? It's a little after office hours."

"So I'm told. I'm also told that you are in possession of a certain set of files, three copies I believe."

Frank gritted his teeth. "I was just thinking about paying you a visit," he replied, "but I decided to let the police do it instead."

"I'll bet you did," Saunders said, "but I would strongly advise against it. You see, I have a couple of your friends with me, and I've convinced them that I'm serious. Here, I'll let you speak with one of them."

"Frank!" Mrs. Rawlson screamed. "He came after me. They forced daddy to tell them about the report. Daddy is very ill, Frank. I'm afraid he's having another heart attack. I—"

There were muffled scuffling sounds, like hands slapping the phone hand set, then, "I'll get to the point, Adams. Two of my men will be stopping by your office in a little while. I want you to be very polite and go with them. And, oh yes, bring those three copies of the files with you."

"What files? What are you talking about?"

"Please, Mr. Adams, don't be asinine. I thought you were more skilled than that. Bring the papers, and don't call the police. If you have already done so, then call them back and take them off the scent. If you decide to pull any fast ones, if we see the slightest sign of a policeman, I'm afraid we'll have to dispose of our two live assets and make an ungraceful departure."

"But—" Frank started to say.

The mechanical buzz in his ear meant the conversation was over.

They were in command now. He couldn't call the police, and there was no way on earth to fake one of the copies. He would have to play along and hope for a chance to salvage the original, which was still in Amertek's safe.

CHAPTER 18

February 23
Friday, 12:15 a.m.

T he major was well into the night shift at the hospital when she received a call from Frank.

"Major, get away early. I need you now. Some gentlemen in dark suits are going to pick me up at my office and take me for a long ride. Park nearby so you've got a clear view of the main entrance to my office. If I can, I'll switch off the lights to let you know when we're coming down. Just keep us in sight. You're the only chance I've got. They're holding Russell and his daughter hostage, and they mean business."

The major took a quick breath. There was something truly close to panic in Frank's voice.

"Don't say anything," Frank said. "There isn't time. Just get over here as fast as you can. Tell them it's a personal emergency, anything, but get over here. I'm going to call that fella Corey—the guy up near my cabin—and tell him what's going on. You remember. He's an ex-cop. He'll help. Call him when you figure out where they have taken me. He'll know what to do."

Frank recited Corey's phone number and had her repeat it twice.

"You got it?"

"Yes," she said, her voice a few notes higher. "Why don't you get outta there now? Why wait for them to come?"

"It's the only way I can get to Russell and his daughter. They want something from me, and they'll hurt them if they don't get it. Hurry!"

Despite her attempt to be careful, the major had scribbled the numbers so that some were unreadable. She tried to call Frank back, but all she got was a busy signal. She tried a few more times, then hung up.

She would have to borrow Dr. Sinclair's car. They hadn't been on the friendliest terms lately, but if she explained that it was an emergency and moved her lips in just the right way, the resident doctor would hand over the keys in an instant.

She found Dr. Sinclair at the nurse's station perusing a patient's chart. She did her eyes just right, the way he liked, very open and girlish. She used her hands, pleading with them, and she did her lips in that way—a sort of opened mouth, full-lipped quiver, like Marilyn Monroe expressing an unspeakable desire. The doctor, his blood vessels throbbing in his temples, pressed the keys into her hand and held them there. The major gently pulled her hand away with the keys.

"Tomorrow night?" he whispered. "You can return them to me in bed."

"Once everything is sorted out. I'll let you know."

He would be over at her place roaring like a rogue elephant. Just her luck that the only person on her shift who could possibly loan her a car was little boy lecher. She would have to wriggle out of it later.

She hurried past the lab and the emergency room, glancing only briefly at the worried faces of people with broken limbs or bleeding wounds waiting in plastic chairs for their turn.

The doctor owned a BMW Z3 in new condition, complete with a collection of "let's get cozy" musical hits. She started the car and immediately felt like she might have awakened the entire neighborhood. The muffler popped and gurgled and made throaty, flapping sounds when she pumped the accelerator.

The windows fogged over, and she reached for a cloth that was tucked behind the seat. It turned out to be a pair of women's panties that she dropped like a poisonous snake. She pulled a clean tissue from her purse and wiped the windshield until it disintegrated into organic fragments in her hand.

The world, seen through the foggy windshield of the doctor's tiny sports car, looked blurred and overwhelming. She found herself looking up at traffic lights, at road signs, and at the rare pedestrian crossing the street. Her ears hummed with stress and adrenaline.

She felt plunged into a sinister, miniature world, like *Alice in Wonderland*. Frank sounded a bit like the White Rabbit. "Hurry up. Hurry up. No time to waste, no time to waste. I'm late. I'm late . . ." But this was no tea party. Frank was in serious trouble.

The major took chances she would never have taken, even with her own car, blowing off the speed limit, charging through yellow traffic lights, and even slipping through a couple of solid reds. Washington was a completely different city after midnight. The few cars left in the city seemed to travel at top speed, darting from one traffic light to the next, dodging around slower obstacles. All seemed to be hurrying somewhere, away from the dark center of the city to its darker extremities.

The major found herself at the lower end of New York Avenue, past the warehouse district and into the old, rundown residential section of the once grand rowhouses and elegant apartments, their broken and shabby exteriors now brightly illuminated by intense mercury vapor lights.

She rounded Mt. Vernon Square and turned right on I Street, traveling as fast as she could within the posted speed limit. She didn't want to be pulled over for speeding. She drove past Frank's office building. The sidewalks were mostly deserted. The front entrance looked empty but lit. A couple walked down the block, arm in arm, holding each other closely. She didn't have time to spot Frank's office window. The BMW Z3 demanded most of her attention.

She circled the block and found a parking space on the corner. She counted the floors up to Frank's office. The lights were still on. She could even see a figure moving, or was it two figures? She folded her arms and nestled down in the seat to stay warm and wait for Frank's signal.

A figure partially covered by a blanket or large overcoat staggered around the corner. He stopped in front of her car, swayed a few times, then stumbled on. She reached over and pushed the lock on the door, but it didn't budge. She hit it with the palm of her hand, then her fist, and finally twisted herself into a position to set several good kicks at it, but nothing moved it. She frantically tried the lock on the other side, and it was immovable too.

That was it. Fear surged. "That bastard, scaring me to death, running around getting himself killed. I'll kill him when I see him," she hissed. Her eyes blurred with tears, and she vowed bitterly that Frank would suffer for scaring her like this.

"Oh, Frank, you goddam bastard, you're gonna pay. You're gonna be sorry you were born, you son of a bitch," she growled brutally as she eyed Frank's window.

She almost missed the black, shiny Lincoln that cruised by Frank's office building and stopped at the intersection in front of her. There were two men in the front seat. The car turned right, accelerated down the street, and in a few moments, came to a momentary stop before turning into the parking garage below Frank's building.

Corey's phone rang at least ten times before Frank gave up. He tried again a few minutes later, but there was no answer, not even an active voicemail. He peered out the window and searched the street below. Nothing unusual. The street was deserted except for a few shadowy, fast-moving figures darting from buildings to cars. They could shoot him on the street, and maybe they would. No one would notice or care, and there was no sign of a cop. He hoped against hope that the major was able to get away from the hospital in time.

He called the hospital's number again. The switchboard operator answered in a robotic voice. He asked for the major's floor and waited as the connections were made. He heard a noise outside. The door to Vickie's reception area was open, and he could see the door to the hall as it burst open and slammed like a stone against the doorstop.

Two very large men stepped in. They were wearing dark suits and sunglasses, with one hand in a side pocket. They did not seem to be in a hurry. One of them slowly pulled out a small revolver and motioned for Frank to put down the phone.

Frank could hear a voice on the other end. How he wished he were on the other end, enveloped in safety at the hospital. He listened to it fade away as he lowered the receiver. At least it didn't sound like the major, so perhaps she had left. There was still some hope.

"Thank you, sir," the man with the gun said. "Now, if you would please hand the materials over to me."

He held out a large hand, calloused and scarred, perhaps from intense practice in martial arts, thought Frank. He made a move to open his desk drawer. The man cocked the hammer on his pistol and pointed it directly at Frank's head.

"I have one copy in here and one in the safe. The other is there," Frank said as he pointed to the large manila envelope on the side of his desk.

"Move no further, sir," the armed man said. "Shazid, see to the desk."

Shazid, the other man, walked behind Frank's desk, shoved him to one side, and opened the center drawer. He triumphantly held up the second envelope and placed it on top of the other.

"Now, the one in the safe, please. Just open the safe door and step away. Shazid will take it from there."

Frank stepped over to the safe, turned the dial, popped the small, thick door open, and stepped back.

"Good," said the man with the gun, as if he were complimenting Frank for having written his name correctly for the first time.

Shazid completed the process by opening the door wide and carefully examining the inside with a flashlight. He reminded Frank of an archaeologist looking into a prehistoric tomb. He removed the contents of the safe, leafed through them, stopped at the manila envelope, and held its contents up for his partner to identify.

The man with the gun nodded, then motioned for Frank to back up against the wall. Frank complied and watched as both men rummaged through his desk, stacking his papers in separate piles. The gunman pulled out Frank's answering machine and portable recorder tapes. He screened the tapes and smiled at Frank as the kidnapper's phone conversation played. Shazid went into the reception area and ransacked Vickie's desk.

They made quick work of it. They knew what they wanted: all correspondence and communication regarding the Rawlson case. He imagined they had already turned over his apartment very thoroughly. They intended to do a clean, professional job. No written proof of his connection with the Rawlsons—no tapes, pictures, nothing would survive. It was becoming obvious what their ultimate plan was for him.

They would arrange something, an accident, a robbery victim, the oldest way of covering up murder and, in Washington, the most believable. Maybe they had arranged something for him at his mountain cabin. Whatever it was, he had silently accepted that he wasn't going to get out of this alive.

He thought about making a break for it, but his friend with the gun and the self-satisfied smile seemed to be waiting for just such an attempt. He would have to get through the reception area, and the other thug would get him. If he got past the door, there was the hall and the elevator. And there was Mrs. Rawlson and her father to consider. There was essentially no way out for him until he got on the street.

The gunman stopped the tape, ran it back, and pushed the buttons that would erase it.

"I'm afraid, Mr. Adams, that the game is over for you. But you have played well, with honor and courage, most unusual for an American. It is too bad."

"Don't you like Americans?"

The man smiled. "Of course. How can one not like Americans? You are such silly people, like children, always playing with toys, and when one of your toys is taken away, you stomp your feet and cry out. And this American democracy of yours, more children's games. You do not understand real power or how to use it. You are like a stupid, happy giant tramping his way through the world. Those who need your help, you ignore or destroy. Those you do help turn out to be monsters in bright uniforms. Yes, my friend, your American heyday is soon coming to an end, and the world will be led by those who know its true ways."

The tape finished erasing with a loud click, and the gunman slipped the device back into the desk drawer. He was no longer smiling. Frank noticed his face looked particularly drawn, as if this ideological diatribe had tapped a vital fluid. *This might be a soft spot*, Frank thought.

"You mind telling me who these people are who know the true ways of the world so well?" Frank asked.

Another harangue might distract him just long enough to make a break for it.

"You will know soon enough, for all the good it will do you."

His voice was hoarse and strained. He wasn't going to be lured into that type of mistake. He acknowledged something from Shazid with a nod.

"It is time to go, Mr. Adams." He waved his gun toward the door.

Frank felt the knots that had been tightening in his abdomen for years start to loosen and slip out one by one. It took all his willpower not to run as they started for the door.

"Wait," Frank said. "Would you mind turning off the lights? The power bills are simply astronomical these days."

One of the gunmen smiled and reached for the light switch. The men kept Frank between them in the hall and in the elevator. Frank's last hope was the night watchman in the lobby, but they took the elevator directly down to the parking garage, and there would be no chance of seeing him there. Frank followed Shazid, focusing on his thick, dark neck and feeling the other man's wet breath on his neck.

They snaked around a few parked cars and stopped at a long, black Lincoln. Shazid opened the back door, and the gunman shoved his weapon into Frank's back.

"Get in," he said.

Frank slid and stumbled into the rear seat, groping his way into what seemed like a richly upholstered cave. Shazid shuffled in beside him, very close. An instant later he felt a sharp stab in his shoulder. He looked at Shazid's grinning face and then, horrified at a hypodermic syringe Shazid was holding.

The gunman got behind the wheel and started the engine. Frank's eyes blurred as the car slowly melted and broke apart into surreal, harmless particles. Frank was adrift, floating in a kind of starless twilight toward a black hole.

CHAPTER 19

The major saw the lights go off in Frank's office. Her fingers tightened on the steering wheel. A little later she saw the big, black Lincoln roll out onto I Street. That had to be it. No one else had entered or left the building since she began her surveillance, and Frank had said that the lights were the signal they were leaving. The limo accelerated past her, and she caught a brief glimpse of the driver's profile. She could see only one man in the front seat. The rear windows were dark, tinted glass.

She started the Z3 and pulled out behind the Lincoln. She had never followed anyone before, so she would have to use her instincts. On television, the follower was always spotted by the one being followed, and then a car chase ensued. But TV seldom told the truth about anything. She hoped the driver of the Lincoln would not risk being stopped by the police.

The major started an internal monologue, mostly to keep herself alert. *If they see me, they'll probably string me along until they can duck undercover. But maybe they won't notice. Washington is a big town, with so many people on the road, even at one in the morning.*

The black Lincoln stopped at a traffic light, and the major stopped close behind it and made a mental note of the license plate. It was an out-of-state tag from New York, with the name of a dealer in chrome lettering surrounding the plate. Manhattan Auto was all she could make out. The rear window was tinted. They were heading north on the Beltway and being very careful to obey every traffic rule. She decided to wait and see if they turned east on Highway 50. If not, she would take a chance and pass them, hoping to throw off suspicion.

They took the exit to Highway 50 east. There were not many turn-offs on that section of the road. It was the main artery in this part of the state to the Bay Bridge, Eastern Shore, and the northeast.

She waited until the few cars joining the highway had merged, then stepped down hard on the little accelerator and buzzed around the Lincoln like a restless college girl with too much of Daddy's money. She knew she had caught the driver's attention and, hopefully, his dismissal. *It was a better move than sticking on his tail for miles. That's a dead giveaway,* she thought.

The major moved several car lengths ahead and slowed down to the speed limit. She stayed like this, at times losing speed or sometimes gaining it, just an ordinary driver on her way home. She gradually dropped behind him again after about twenty miles.

The black Lincoln passed her moving at a steady fifty-five miles per hour. The car reminded her of a hearse: silent, dark, self-contained, and strangely isolated among the living vehicles on the road. She dropped back even more, gaining distance, and allowed another car in front of her. The Lincoln's right turn signal was blinking. He was going to go over the bridge across the Chesapeake. She paid the bridge toll in the booth next to the Lincoln. She delayed, pretending to be searching for toll money, until she saw the Lincoln move out of the gate. She quickly handed the attendant the correct amount and sped away from the toll gate. She swung in behind a large panel truck where she could see the Lincoln in the right lane of the bridge. She was not out of sight of the big car but, she hoped, it was not obvious either.

The wake of an oncoming eighteen-wheeler passing by tore at the car's soft top, and the wind at the top of the bridge kept bouncing her to the right. She passed a small flag—or was it a windsock—mounted near one of the bridge lights. It stood straight out, fluttering like a high-frequency tuning fork. Even the bridge itself seemed to move. Snow and ice at the top of the bridge seemed to be slowly giving way to the wind, like the top of a mountain slowly eroding.

The Z3 skidded on the surface at the center of the bridge. The major's heart froze for a second, but she was careful not to overcorrect. The pavement must be accumulating ice. It felt like she had hit an oil spot. The eighteen-wheeler had no trouble; it could blast and bust its way through anything.

They were on the downside now, almost coasting toward the Eastern Shore, a world of prosperous farms, historic towns, broad, flat fields, and horse farms intermingled with summer homes for the Washington, Baltimore, and Philadelphia gentry. There was a serenity about the place that always got on her nerves. Everyone seemed to have all the time in the world.

The Lincoln took Highway 301 North for about fifteen miles, then turned left down a rough narrow county road. The green sign read Queen's Road, as the major's headlights flashed past it. This would be the giveaway.

She turned into the first driveway she saw and switched off her lights, including her instrument lights. She waited a few moments, then backed quickly out onto the road. She would follow their rear lights close enough so that she would not lose them.

It was a very dangerous stunt, and if she allowed herself to think about it for very long, little fingers of fear crawled over her scalp. She had to fight the fear; that was all there was to it. She had to know where they were taking Frank. She couldn't give him up to the wolves now.

She was relieved it was so late and a winter night. There was hardly another car to be seen, no early rising farmers starting the day's work, no casual joggers or deliverymen. The one thing she worried about was hitting a deer crossing the road in front of her invisible car. Or even a squirrel. She didn't know if she could take that. She hoped, even muttered a little prayer, that it would not happen.

The land around here was low, thickly wooded in places, and sometimes swampy. Something appeared in front of her, an amoeba-shaped body blurring the red taillights ahead. She was in it before she could step on the brakes. She suppressed a scream. In an instant, she was out of it. She glanced in the rearview mirror but saw nothing. Some creeping cloud of frozen mist. "What the fuck is next?" she growled between her teeth.

She needed to get more control of herself. Driving without lights on a black night with adrenaline pumping was draining. She forced herself to focus hard on the red taillights in front of her. She could not judge distances very well, and it was hard to tell when they slowed down or accelerated. It seemed like a long, dark tunnel. There was little physical sensation of speed, yet she knew she was moving quite fast over the narrow road. The only indication that she was in a moving vehicle was the sound of the wind whistling through the cracks in the car and the sound of tires thumping on the asphalt.

The red taillights were approaching rapidly. She gingerly tapped the small brake pedal; fearful they would notice the brake lights glowing faintly in their rearview mirror. It wasn't enough to stop the car, so she pumped the brakes, sending her into an oscillating skid. It looked like she was going to collide with Frank's kidnappers.

She reached for the light switch, feeling around the pitch-black instrument panel like a blind woman trying to find the right knob. She patted the panel wildly, and just as she found the knob, the limo abruptly made a sharp right turn. Deciding to remain in the dark a bit longer, she coasted past the point where the car turned and gradually came to a stop, threw the car into reverse, and continued to follow them.

When the red taillights came into view, she slowed to a crawl. They were receding fast, bouncing, and trailing large vortices of brown, glowing dust. She could not see well enough to risk turning around, so she waited for the taillights to disappear. Roads were straighter in this flat part of the state. They could go for miles before turning. She waited. The lights moved closer together and to the left as they distanced themselves from her, then vanished.

She restrained herself for a few moments. Then, with a tremendous effort of will and a little more hand searching, she switched on her headlights. The whole countryside around her lit up. Ice-covered tree branches glistened around her like a gargantuan web.

A large black iron gate, supported by heavy brick columns, blocked the gravel road that the Lincoln had taken. Brick walls extended out on either side of the columns for fifty feet and became a continuous chain-link fence with overhanging razor wire at the top.

She guessed this structure surrounded the property, and the gate was probably operated by a remote transmitter. There were no obvious signs of CCTV cameras, but she couldn't be sure. The razor wire atop the brick wall gave the appearance of a prison to what was clearly a wealthy estate.

There was a white square of masonry on one of the columns flanking the gates that might have once held the name of the place, but it appeared blank in the gloom. There was nothing else the major could see that would even hint at an address.

She jotted down the mileage of the Z3, turned around, and drove slowly back to the main road. She headed the way she had come, watching eagerly for road signs or anything that would tell her where she was. She needed to know that before calling the number Frank had given her.

There was little indication that there were other living people in the world until she was back on Highway 301. She wrote down the mileage distance to the intersection and felt something close to hysterical joy when she spotted at an all-night truck stop. She pulled snugly up beside an eighteen-wheeler.

The man she assumed to be the driver was sitting inside the restaurant at an otherwise vacant counter, sipping coffee and smoking a short cigar despite the "no smoking" signs. The major entered quickly to give the impression that she was in a hurry and expecting someone.

"Could you tell me where I am?" she asked halfway across the counter to a disheveled, sleep-deprived waitress.

A truck driver, several seats away, beamed a broad smile at her.

"I must have taken a wrong turn somewhere," the major said to the waitress.

"Sure thing, honey," the truck driver responded. "Now don't you worry." He took her hand in both of his. She quickly pulled her hand away.

The trunk driver continued smiling, as if he expected this reaction. "Where do you want to go, darlin'?" he asked.

"I was supposed to meet a friend after I got off duty. I'm new to the area and—"

The truck driver turned around on his stool and crushed out his cigar. He had lost interest. Not much of a pursuer. The waitress watched them anxiously for a moment until she was sure her customers had reached an understanding. Then, moving closer, she said to the major, "You can tell your boyfriend you're at the Midway Inn on 301, honey."

She threw a glance at the truck driver and twisted the side of her mouth in a grimace for the major to see—a woman-to-woman signal that the guy was trouble. The major smiled, said "thank you," and reached into her purse for her cell phone. She punched in Corey's number, hoping that she read her scribble correctly. It rang several times before Corey's heavy, sleepy voice answered. She quickly explained who she was and reminded him of their meeting just a few days ago. The waitress and the truck driver were engaged in a buzzing conversation over the counter. In a hushed voice, she told Corey what had happened, only mentioning the important points.

Corey, now fully awake, said he would be there in about two and a half hours. Could she wait? "Yes," she said as she thought about the hospital and all the sleep, she was going to lose in the next twenty-four hours.

She went back to the counter and looked at a menu encased in a yellow, greasy plastic cover. The truck driver gave her a quick glance, slid from his stool, and headed outside to his truck. The waitress wiped the place on the counter that he had occupied with several swirls of a stained, damp cloth, tossed it in an unseen place under the counter, and ambled toward the major.

"Gonne have to wait, huh?" the waitress said.

The major nodded.

"Ain't that the way it always is? No matter what they say about this woman's lib stuff making us free and independent and all, we always end up waiting on some man. I mean, if we could just find a way of living without 'em. But you know, honey, next to starving to death, sleeping alone in a cold bed is about the worst thing that can happen to you. And, honey, even after you have the operation to have it all cut out, it still don't stop wantin' it."

The waitress laughed, indifferently exposing her stained and blackened teeth. She leaned closer. "After my old man left me for the third time, a girlfriend of mine sent me one of those vibrator things." She snickered. "So now when a man starts giving me the hassle, I just pull that thing out of its box and dangle it in front of him." She held up an imaginary device and waved it in front of the major's face. Then she slapped the counter with both hands and guffawed until her hoarse smoker's laughter turned into uncontrollable coughing followed by one or two violent hiccups.

The major smiled and ordered the Four Wheelers breakfast.

It was growing light outside when she saw a brown, mud-splattered pick-up truck park next to the BMW. Its headlights were paled a little by the morning light. Corey walked toward the entrance of the rest stop. She was surprised at his physical size, almost frightened by it.

The waitress followed him with glittering eyes. Once inside, Corey smiled in an appreciative acknowledgment. He slipped off his heavy wool parka and sat down on the stool beside the major.

"Let's get two coffees and that corner table over there, and you can tell me everything you know."

CHAPTER 20

February 23
Friday, morning

F rank gradually became aware of a great drum beating louder and louder, making him more aware of something physically real: the bed he was lying on, distant windows, a table, chairs, a vase of flowers and, above, a glassy reflection of himself sprawled grotesquely on a velvet bedspread. He rose on his elbows and looked around. The drumming had slowed to a steady pain in the center of his head and seemed to dissolve parts of his brain every time he moved. He managed to move to the side of the bed and sit, putting his feet unsteadily on the floor.

Thick carpet sprang up around his shoes. Gold flashed from all parts of the room. The chairs were from the fifteenth century Italian Renaissance and gilt like the picture frames. A pair of rose medallion Chinese floor vases, probably Qing dynasty, flanked the windows. Even the wall coverings were opulent with gold-on-gold damask.

Frank stood up, waited a few moments for the pain to ebb, then slowly edged his way to the wall to examine the pictures. They were original oils, mostly eighteenth and nineteenth century, signed illegibly, but showed training and talent. One wall had portraits, possibly of the founders of the plantation. Another wall housed a collection of Mughal miniatures that would be the envy of any museum.

Frank turned his attention to more practical concerns and approached the highly polished windows, which bore the wavy imperfections typical of eighteenth-century glass. Outside, the grounds were covered in pale, frosted winter grass and rolled gently to a line of tall, bare trees and a tall brick wall beyond that. There was a large swimming pool near the house that was covered for the winter, and to the right, there was a cluster of farm buildings. Far to the left, a sliver of dazzling light indicated a large body of water.

He looked at his watch. He had been out for six hours, which was enough time to cover a lot of territory. He was reasonably sure of the general area, probably a remote part of Maryland's Eastern Shore judging from the flat landscape and the glimpse of water to the west. But he could also be in some parts of Virginia or even New Jersey.

The sequence of events of last night gradually filtered back to him. Questions flooded his mind. Who was holding him? Were Russell and Mrs. Rawlson here too? How would he get three people out of here? Even if he could escape, leaving them behind was as good as a death sentence. If there was a way out for him, it had to work for all of them.

On impulse, he examined the window. It slid open effortlessly. He stood in front of the open window, feeling the cold air blasting in. Resisting the chance at freedom, he took a deep breath and closed the window.

"A very wise move, Mr. Adams."

The quiet male voice came from a hidden speaker on the opposite wall.

"It's very encouraging to know that you are not a complete fool. It's very tempting, isn't it? All you have to do is open the window and climb down using a bed sheet, or perhaps a drainpipe, although I certainly would not trust that.

"We would have had some fun with you first. My friends insist on that. Then we would have to forcibly bring you back, unconscious of course. Look in the corner opposite you. You'll see a small lens. It always keeps an impartial eye on you. There is no way to avoid it, so please don't try. If you do, one of the household staff will be forced to investigate, and they are usually extremely angry when they have to do that. So, get as much rest as you can, enjoy the view. See you soon."

Frank looked around the room in search of the camera. It was mounted on the ceiling and attached to a swivel. It looked like a large, black eyeball always looking at him.

"What's happened to Mr. Russell and Helen Rawlson? Where are they?"

The speaker was silent. Frank knew it would be useless to ask again. They were in complete control, whoever they were. He would have to wait for a good opportunity, a mistake in their programming, but their planning had been faultless so far. Except for the needle that Shazid jabbed into his arm, the last thing Frank remembered seeing was a streetlight, and the last thing he remembered feeling was a desperate desire to hang on to that light. He didn't feel anger, regret, or even panic. He had just wanted to keep seeing that streetlight.

He wasn't dead, however, and he wasn't going to let himself think about it. Not now, not while he was alive and feeling a tremendous pain in his head. He was going to get out of this somehow. The major was still out there. Even if she couldn't contact Corey, or if she hadn't been able to follow Frank and his kidnappers, at least she was still out there and knew he was in trouble. She would do something. She would not let him go under.

Frank knew this kind of thinking would soon drive him to some desperate or stupid act. He would have to assume the major could not help. It would be completely up to him.

He looked up at the camera, which was watching him like a reptilian eye. He approached the bed. The eye followed, its iris rotating for the sharpest focus. Maybe they were lying. He had not seen anyone on the grounds. It appeared to be a huge estate, but he knew there were at least three men on the other side of the room.

On an impulse, he ran for the window, threw it open, and looked down at the twenty-foot drop. He swung one leg out the window when the door burst open, and a pair of hands grabbed his shirt and yanked him back into the room. They spun him around. The man locked Frank's arms behind his back and held him around the neck, allowing just enough air in his lungs to keep him from passing out. A man with a gun, the same one from the night before, stood in front of him, smiling gleefully as he shoved his hand into a black leather glove.

"Very, very disappointing, Mr. Adams," he said. "You should have taken my word. Shazid, we must show Mr. Adams that we are quite serious."

"I agree, Ahmet. Shall we use the medication?"

"Don't be silly, my friend. That is for a higher purpose. It is for later."

Ahmet, still smiling, held his gloved hand over Frank's eyes, waited a few moments, then buried his other fist into Frank's midsection, just below the ribs. Frank pitched forward against the hold of Shazid and went limp.

"Let him fall to the floor," said Ahmet.

Shazid released his grip on Frank's arms. Frank crumpled to the floor like an oversized water balloon, as he struggled to breathe and not throw up. He felt himself slipping into unconsciousness and tried to fight against it, but soon everything was dark and quiet.

CHAPTER 21

February 23
Friday, 11:20 a.m.

F rank first became aware of the woolly, antiseptic smell of the carpet, then the stabbing pain as if piano wire were tightening around his chest. He could only take shallow half-breaths before the pain stopped him. His head throbbed, and it felt like his last meal had been pushed back up into his throat.

Slowly, his memory returned. He got to his feet and stumbled toward the bed. He lay atop the red-and-gold bedspread for a long time, trying to suppress panic in his fight for air. He looked up. The camera eye had followed, of course. It knew every move he made.

"I have to use the bathroom," he tried to call out, but the words came out as more of a croak. He heard a metallic snap and a door at the end of the room swung open. Frank struggled off the bed and staggered toward the door.

The bathroom was very elaborate. There were gold-plated fixtures, including a bidet, decorated with erotic figures. Frank tried to close the door, but it wouldn't budge.

"What do you think I'm going to do in here? Or do you get your kicks from watching?" he said in a choking voice as he glared at the camera eye.

The hold on the door was released, creating an atmosphere

like a charged plasmatic field surrounding it. Frank moved the door back and forth a few times to see if it was actually free, then closed it.

He knelt over the bidet and threw up into it. The pain caused everything to darken for a moment, but he held on to the bidet until his vision began to clear. He dry-heaved a few times, then sat on the toilet seat and wiped his foul-tasting mouth with toilet paper. He looked down and realized he had soiled his pants. It must have happened when Ahmet let him have it in the umbilical region.

He opened the door and said, "I need a change of clothes," though he wasn't quite able to express his rage. Then he went back to the bathroom, stripped off his filthy clothes, and turned on the shower.

He took a long shower. The water was wonderfully hot, and he let it course over his body in a thousand hot rivulets. The hot water seemed to restore some of his energy and even alleviated some of the constant pain.

He left the shower water running when he stepped out and tossed his pants in. They would have to be cleaned first, then the rest of his foul-smelling clothes. When he finished scouring them, he threw them back out onto the white tiled floor and stayed in the shower for a few happy minutes longer.

He dried off slowly with one of the large, fluffy towels, wrapped it around his waist, and tossed the long free end over his shoulder like a Roman toga.

A long-sleeved T-shirt and a pair of clean, pressed, military-type coveralls were laid out on the bed when he returned from the shower, as well as a meal of some kind of grain or couscous. He slipped into the coveralls—they were a size too large—and sat on the edge of the bed to sample the food. It tasted a little like cornmeal mixed with some type of meat flavoring. But it was hot, and despite throwing up only minutes before, it felt good to have something warm and nourishing in his stomach again.

He finished the contents of the bowl and lay back on the bed. The pains were slowly subsiding. He didn't believe his ribs were fully broken. He had broken ribs before, and the pain never let up. A strange feeling of contentment came over him. He let his head sink back into the pillow. He didn't mind the room. He didn't even object to the camera constantly trained on him. He felt like he could spend the rest of his life in this room, as long as they served him hot meals and gave him clean clothes.

A warm, fluid sleep began to wash over him—a good, sound sleep. Even the thought that he might soon die didn't bother him. The call to sleep, or death, was too powerful, too seductive to resist. He gave in, let himself go, and somewhere in the twilight semiconsciousness of pre-sleep, the bedroom door burst open. He heard it, but felt no alarm, not even when he opened his eyes a little wider and saw the bearded face of Ahmet standing over him. Ahmet's accomplice was behind him, looking stone-faced as usual.

"Wake up, fool! I want you awake!" Ahmet said, half-smiling as he swiftly drew a long, double-edged knife from his jacket. Frank lunged clumsily at the men before he could shake off the drug effects of sleep. Ahmet took a step back, ripped open the lower part of Frank's coveralls, and placed the cold edge of the knife against his genitals. The pain felt like a kick in the stomach. He sat up and rested on his elbows. The pain sharpened, almost cutting.

"One more move and I'll make you a eunuch! What a dog you are. What a coward. A man of my country would not allow himself to be so treated. You American men are nothing. You are a nation of women."

"If you're going to cut my balls off, go ahead and do it. But please spare me the political harangue, will you?" Frank said, surprised at his recklessness.

Ahmet slowly withdrew the knife. "When the time comes, I will. But unfortunately, you are needed for other things. Make yourself presentable. Then come with us. And please try to control your bowels."

"Then don't kick me in the gut," Frank said.

Frank refastened the lower part of his coveralls and sat up on the edge of the bed. Shazid dragged him to his feet and shoved him toward the door and out into the hallway. He had a hawk's grip on Frank's arm, and Ahmet followed behind, occasionally jabbing him in the lower back with the knife handle. Frank was busy counting the doors to figure out the layout.

They stopped in front of a large oak-paneled door. Ahmet pressed an ivory button twice. When the door opened, Frank was pushed into a large conference room with soft lighting and a thick, green carpet. A large oval conference table occupied the center of the room. There were only two chairs, one at each end of the table. Saunders was seated at one end. He was leaning back in the chair as though he was very comfortable and familiar with the place.

"I thought I recognized your voice on the phone," Frank said.

"I was sure you did. But by then, it didn't matter."

"I was going to pay you another visit," Frank said.

"Yes, I anticipated that."

"So, you went by the old man's place to pick up the report with your original initials on it?" Frank said.

Saunders's eyes narrowed. "That will be all for now, Ahmet. I'll buzz you when I'm finished." He made a motion of dismissal with his hand. Ahmet bowed slightly and left the room with his assistant. Saunders hesitated a long time before speaking.

"Have a seat, please," he said politely.

"No, thank you," Frank said.

Saunders shrugged. "Suit yourself, but you may regret it later."

"I doubt it. I know what your plans are for me."

Saunders feigned being surprised. "And what are they?"

"You have all the incriminating reports. You've either killed or captured everyone who can testify against you. What I don't understand is why your boys didn't kill me on the way over here. They certainly wanted to."

Saunders nodded. "They are good soldiers. They do as they're told. But you are wrong about our plans for you and our other two guests. We intend to keep you alive, at least until we have everything we need."

Frank remained silent as he wondered where Mr. Russell and Mrs. Rawlson were being held, and if they, too, were being manhandled by the two thugs.

"You see, until you came on the scene, nobody knew anything, and as such, nobody had to die. Amertek shares went way down, we lost the Dongan contract, the shares went up, and we found MVD Industries, the London-based firm. And everybody got rich. Well, that is to say, I got rich, because my 'partner' Charlie is dead."

Saunders leaned forward and rested his elbows on the table. "But then you had to go snooping around, and I think you know a lot more than you should, and you talked to many more people than you should have. So, what we want to know from you is who you have talked to about this case and how much."

"If I told you that I haven't said a word to anyone, would you believe me?" Frank asked.

Saunders looked thoughtful as he leaned back in his chair. He made a tent with his fingers. "We checked out your secretary . . . Vickie? That's her name, right? It was smart of you not to involve her any more than you did because I really do think she had no idea what we were talking about. However, I doubt if she will show up to work tomorrow. We also had a look at your friends at the NTSB. Now there's a tough bunch. But apparently Sal had done an excellent job, and the damage obliterated any evidence that the crash was anything other than an accident resulting from pilot error. But there are others, we suspect.

"For example, where did you stay the week after Sal's unfortunate death? We know you were with someone. We kept your apartment and office under constant surveillance. We checked every motel and whorehouse in the area. You were safe somewhere, Mr. Adams. All I want to know is where you were and who you were with."

Frank pressed his lips together and resisted the overwhelming urge to leap over Saunders's desk and go for his throat. "I was at my mother's," he seethed.

"What do you think this is, a *James Bond* movie? You are not the stuff that heroes like that are made of." Saunders pounded the conference table with his fist before regaining control and settling back in his chair. "Now, we can settle this sensibly, or I can turn you over to Ahmet. He is very good with drug therapy. When your physical resistance is low enough, we will find out the truth. You can bet on it."

"You won't believe me regardless of what I say," Frank said. "I could say that I didn't tell anyone, and you'd still torture me. But the NTSB already thinks it was an accident. It's over. You got rid of Rawlson, and he's out of your way. I can't prove it was you, and the cops won't care."

Saunders forced a theatrical laugh. "Oh, it's not over. You see, this plan only works if it is completely contained within itself. And you, my friend, are the only outside player who knows too much. With your people 'contained,' we are free to grab our spoils and go. So even if I believe you, there are others who may be skeptical. We must make sure. You understand. I could summon my colleagues to help you recall."

"Okay, okay," said Frank, keen to avoid another visit from the heavy enforcers and buy some time. "All right, correct me if I'm wrong. You and the devoted son-in-law team up for a little power grab. You both know the company is doing well. Several important bids were going out, which, if accepted, would not only mean economic growth but a considerable increase in the profit margin, new markets, big investors. But there was something else."

Saunders grinned and gestured for Frank to continue.

"You two cooked up a plan to reduce the price of the company and close in for the kill. Which, I believe, is still illegal and carries with it several years in prison. So, you created a phony quality control report that would have cost the company millions in recalls and replacements. It would have also shot down the bid for the government contracts. The company's value would plummet, and since you're not a publicly traded company, you don't have to report this. However, a controlled leak to some of the financial journals would do the trick.

"You paid off Sal to write the report and bum up some samples to make it look good to the old man. Charles presented Russell with the report and the doctored equipment. He offered to keep it quiet long enough for the bids to come in, but he demanded more power and authority in the form of a large percentage of the company's shares. He promised to transfer half to you. Charles probably offered to handle the report, saying 'he'd take care of it,' knowing the old man would rather ignore it. Russell has been showing signs of his age lately, hasn't he? Like most kings past their time, Russell preferred to believe what his trusted son-in-law told him, unaware that he was being usurped. So, you let the news leak about the report to some influential friends in the financial districts, only you didn't tell them that it was pure fiction. There was a big sell-off. That's when you and your friends moved in for the takeover. Am I right so far?"

Saunders nodded his head.

"At some point, your plans diverged from Charles's plan. Actually, you never intended to share the profits with him, did you? You've hated Charles all along. You knew Amertek is a family-owned company, and you'd never rise above the beloved son-in-law in the company hierarchy. You also wanted revenge for him pawing your boyfriend."

Frank hesitated for a moment to see if his analysis was having any effect on Saunders.

Saunders's face was expressionless. "Go on," he said. "Please continue. It's fascinating."

"Did anyone else know that Charles was bisexual? Or was that a little piece of blackmail you held over his head so he would go along with your plan? Yes, it's starting to make sense now. So, when the son-in-law dutifully did his part, you paid Sal to take him out. But there's something else. Something doesn't fit. Who are these fanatical thugs with the strange names? And whose compound is this?"

Saunders smiled, and Frank would have mistaken it for a look of inner contentment had it not been for Saunders's steel-pointed eyes.

"As I said earlier, if you had not interfered, Mr. Russell would be naively enjoying his palatial home at this very minute, and Helen would be free to lure any man she wanted into her bed. I must admit, when I learned that Helen had called in an investigator, I only figured you as a possible temporary hindrance."

"But you bungled the job with Sal," Frank said. He was trying to remember what had rattled Saunders in their previous conversations. He wanted to buy time.

Saunders raised his eyebrows, wrinkled his forehead, and his right hand made a fist, his knuckles glowing white.

"Bungled? We didn't bungle anything!" Saunders yelled, and then he gathered his composure. "We did have to improvise. But, as you see, it turned out all right."

Saunders leaned back in his chair and assumed the air of a board chairman. "You are mostly right. We did plan a takeover, but not in the conventional sense. A company like Amertek is an anachronism in today's business world. It was only a matter of time before one of the conglomerates took it over. Charles and I had planned to push the old man out, then sell to the highest bidder. We scared the hell out of the old man with that phony report, and it worked. But after seeing how easy it was, Charles started to get greedy. He had notions of an empire, that sort of thing. And not only that, but he seemed to want it all for himself.

"I started getting bad vibes that things weren't going exactly as I had planned. Then I started feeling a kind of avoidance radiating from other executives, especially from their wives. They began dodging me, a sure sign that you're about to get the axe." Saunders brought his open palm down in a chopping motion.

"Couldn't you have held the phony report over him?"

"I considered it, but my criminal complicity would easily be established. I would have been truly up the creek." Saunders sighed. "As for your other question, that was a stroke of luck regarding Ahmet and Shazid. A miracle happened. Yes, Mr. Adams, I believe in miracles."

Frank did not react but remained expressionless.

Saunders continued. "I have some important friends around Washington. One day, I was approached by Mr. Hosseini, an agent representing MVD Industries, a small but very prosperous investment firm based in London. He explained that his firm was interested in buying a controlling interest in Amertek Electronics.

Something about a missile project. They wanted seventy percent and would cut me in too. I told them it was sure to be rejected by the owners. The agent had heard the founder's son-in-law was ambitious and might be receptive to the proposal, so I promised to speak to Charles. I did and got the reply I expected: knee-slapping laughter. I told this to the agent the next time I saw him. He offered to finance Charles's 'disposal.'"

"At first, I was shocked. I really was. But then he offered me two million dollars, twenty percent control, and the CEO position at Amertek. So, yes, as you say, at that point my plans diverged from Charles's. You know the rest. I put Hosseini in touch with Sassavitte, and when I found out Charles's widow had hired you, all I had to do was say the word, and they sent me several of their best men—trained insurgents, as you see. But the first priority was to deal with Sal."

"They screwed that up, didn't they?" Frank said.

Saunders ignored the comment. "There was another unfortunate mistake with the man in your apartment—one of those human factors. But I must say, you handled it very well. Just another Washington suicide: no obvious clues or traces. You can think on your feet, Mr. Adams. I'll give you that."

"And then I was introduced to a wonderful new drug," Saunders said.

"What drug?" Frank asked.

"Oh, you will see. We will show you what it does, maybe even give you a personal demonstration. It has the unique ability to wipe away memory. It can dissolve short and long-term memory, maybe as far back as childhood. The subject must be taught everything over again: how to read and write his ABCs, how to walk. He even has to be potty trained all over again. Isn't that something? It was developed in Eastern Europe for the humane treatment of, shall we say, awkward people? Political prisoners, agitators, journalists, anyone unwelcome in that former Soviet republic. I think it's called amneopian-2. Don't know what the side effects are, but does it really matter? Very clever, don't you think?"

"Fascinating," Frank said, failing to disguise his sarcasm. "You know, of course, that this foreign investment company is nothing more than a shell company set up by the Iranian government to gain access to American military-grade hardware."

Saunders shrugged. "It's the color of their money I'm interested in, and, shall I say, the opportunity to be in charge."

"You won't be in charge, Saunders. They'll be pulling your strings the entire time, and if you don't jump when they pull, you'll end up going back to play school, and I doubt they'll bother to potty train you or teach you to walk."

Saunders laughed. "Oh, you are so dramatic. Someone told me that you had been an amateur actor, and I can believe it." Saunders narrowed his eyes and leaned forward. "I know what I'm doing. Now, I want the names and addresses of anyone you have talked to about this case, please."

"I've told you the truth."

Suddenly, Saunders lurched forward and slammed his fists on the table. "Very well. You have one hour to think about it, and voluntarily give us the information or we move on to the next phase."

He reached under the table and held his hand there for a few moments. Then the conference room door opened, and Ahmet entered with his assistant.

"Please escort Mr. Adams back to his room."

Shazid grabbed Frank and pulled him back to the door, pushed him through it, and continued pushing until they reached his room. Ahmet pressed Frank against the door by his neck, exerting just enough thumb pressure on Frank's carotid artery to keep him somewhere between twilight and total darkness.

"Apparently you were very foolish in there," Ahmet said, cutting his dark eyes toward the conference room. "That means I will be given the opportunity of persuading you, a task I will perform diligently and with love in my heart."

"I don't get it, Ahmet," Frank managed to choke out. "Why are you taking orders from him, a degenerate, immoral, opportunity-seeking American?"

Ahmet grinned. His hold on Frank's neck loosened. "He is necessary for our purposes, for now. To gain respect from the world one must occasionally crawl with the unclean. We will serve him for as long as we need him."

"And then?" Frank asked.

Ahmet widened his grin. "And then we will no longer need him."

Shazid snickered and reached behind Frank to open the door. Frank, helped by a hard push from Ahmet, fell backward into his room. He lay on his back for a long time, looking up at the ceiling, following the intricate details of the carved patterns. They all seemed to converge on the crystal chandelier in the center. The chandelier sparkled like a thousand frozen teardrops in the direct sunlight that streamed through the windows. Frank could have lost himself in the chandelier's glittering, tinkling wonderland if it had not been for a sudden burst of sunlight in his eyes.

He rolled over and pushed himself to his feet. A glance over his shoulder confirmed that the ever-vigilant black mechanical eye was still on him. He walked over to the windows. The sun was still high but, on its way down. It would settle over the trees as an orange/red ball in a few hours. He wondered if he would be alive by then. Even if the story of the amnesia drug was true, he doubted they would keep him alive. They couldn't afford an epidemic of unexplained total memory loss.

They would reserve that treatment for someone they needed to keep alive. The only chance he had was to keep his mouth shut for as long as he could. They would get the information out of him sooner or later. Ahmet would have his fun first, then they would probably use drugs, then the lethal injection. He looked out over the strange, paradoxically beautiful snow-covered lawn and thought about the major and Corey. He seemed to have known them in another life, as remote and out of touch as the people whose portraits hung on the walls around him.

He stared at the portraits. His thoughts turned to the original owners of the property. Gentlemen and ladies of past centuries, subject to, and likely believers in, a restored English monarchy, and self-vindicating slave owners. Their most advanced technology consisted of wooden turn-about gadgets and hand-forged metal. If they thought about the moon or planets at all, it was probably with superstition or with some elementary scientific knowledge. The painter made sure to depict the rich colors and textures of their clothing and the size and placement of their jewels and badges, as well as their haughty, arrogant faces. He made them look handsome and beautiful, and vitally important.

Saunders's voice blurted out from the wall speaker. "Your time is close to expiring, Mr. Adams. Have you made a decision?"

Frank looked up at the camera and said, "Sorry. I've told you everything."

He expected the door to burst open and Ahmet to rush in, grinning with sadistic lust. But nothing happened. He stood in the center of the room as orange sunlight from the windows reached slowly across the carpet. Then he heard movement outside.

Someone turned the doorknob and opened it. Ahmet wheeled in an old man slouched in a wheelchair. Roused from his stupor by the movement, the old man looked up quizzically at Frank.

"I will leave you two to become reacquainted. I'm sure you will have much to talk about twenty years from now, but you only have one minute. That is all," Ahmet said, and he left the room.

Frank knelt beside the wheelchair. "Mr. Russell, what have they done to you?"

He took the old man's hand in his. His pulse was weak, and his palm was a bit moist. Then Frank took his head gently in his hands and lifted it.

"Mr. Russell, do you remember me? Frank Adams."

The old man's eyes were as wide and vacant as a newborn infant. Long drops of clear saliva fell from his lower lip.

"Mr. Russell, can you tell me anything? Is your daughter all right?"

Mr. Russell started to cry, the desperate, demanding cry of a baby.

Frank looked up at the camera. "You son of a bitch!" he screamed. "You're nothing but a common traitor to your country, Saunders. And your henchmen here hate traitors almost as much as they hate Americans." "Ahmet!" Frank shouted toward the camara. "He'll betray you. He's way ahead of all of you, and he'll turn you in. Trust me."

Saunders's voice shouted from the speaker, "If you don't want to see Mrs. Rawlson in that condition, you had better come across with the information we want. And now!"

CHAPTER 22

February 24
Saturday, 6:30 a.m.

"**A**re you sure Frank was in that car?" Corey asked in a way that expected complete honesty.

"Yes," the major said. "I'm sure."

"Okay," Corey said, "Let's go." He stood up.

"Go where?"

"There is a small airport a few miles from here: East Bay Shore airport. I thought we might get a bird's-eye view of where Frank is being held before we go busting in, an aerial reconnaissance if you will."

"That sounds like a good idea."

The major got up from the table. Corey reached into his pocket.

"Hey, it's on me," the major insisted, and left the money in plain sight on the table.

The airport looked deserted. Boulders of icy snow were banked into two-foot walls along each side of the runway. Long icicles hung from the wings and tail surfaces on the airplanes. Tiedown ropes sagged from the weight of the ice, and sunlight glittered in the softening frost that covered everything like a thin sprinkling of glass.

"It doesn't look like much is going on," the major said.

Corey walked to the door of the office. He read the small sign in the window, then looked at his watch. "They open in a little over an hour." he said. "Tell you what, I'm still not sure where Frank is being held. Why don't you show me the way by road? If we can find it on the highway map, then it'll be no trouble spotting it from the air."

The major opened the door to the Z3.

"Why don't we go in my truck?" Corey suggested. "No need to take both vehicles."

"I may not be able to recognize it. Everything looks so different from inside one of those." She pointed to his truck. Corey smiled and shrugged. He walked over to the passenger side of the Beamer, opened the door, and squeezed into the seat.

"You look like an encapsulated man," the major said as she placed her gloved hand over her mouth to cover her smile.

"That is exactly what I feel like." He closed the door.

"I feel like I'm riding with a great and, I hope, tame bear," the major said.

Corey looked over at her, smiling. "Very tame, and do you want to know the truth?"

"Yes."

"I've always wanted to ride in one of these miniature cars."

"Then let's go." She started the engine, backed up, and rolled out onto the road.

They drove for twenty minutes with Corey reading the road map and directing the major to turn here or turn there until finally they passed a place that came closest to fitting the major's description. It was a large Edwardian style mansion with an oak-tree lined driveway. There was also a formidable brick wall along the front of the property with a large, black iron gate. The gate was locked with a chain.

"I've seen enough." Corey said.

When they arrived back at the airport, another car, an old model Ford, sagging on its springs, was parked next to Corey's truck.

The office door was open. They walked in. A man was peering intently at the wall thermostat and turned it. A furnace came on with what sounded like a dangerous explosion. With an expectation of heat, the man rubbed his hands eagerly together and seemed embarrassed when he looked over and saw the major and Corey standing there watching him.

"I hate the cold, and this is the coldest goddamn place on earth. I'm convinced of it. Can I help you?" he said, rubbing his hands together.

"Yes," Corey said. "We would like to look at some property near here. Could someone fly us over it?"

"I don't see why not, provided we can get the bird started. It just doesn't like to go in this kind of weather. I bought it from an outfit shop in Florida, and it just can't take it here. I know how it feels."

The major looked at Corey as if to suggest they look for another airport.

Seeing her glance, the man said reassuringly, "I'll take you. Why don't you wait here while I get the engine preheater going. Then you can tell me what you want to see."

The man left through a side door that opened into a hangar.

The man returned after a few minutes, still rubbing his hands vigorously together. "It'll take a little more time before the engine oil returns to a more liquid state. Now, where did you want to go?"

Corey took out his road map and drew a circle around the general area. "I can only recognize the place from this road," he said, pointing at an area on the map with his pen. "How low can you go?"

The pilot frowned. "I can get down to five hundred feet in that area, but any lower, the neighbors tend to complain, and I could get into trouble with the feds."

"Good. That will do. And we may want to look at it from, say, a thousand feet."

"Fine. Anything you say. Just let me know when you see it."

Corey and the major followed the pilot to the hangar when he finished filing a local flight plan at his desk. They waited next to the door of the airplane while the pilot quickly switched off the preheater and disconnected the heating ducts that went into the cowling.

"It's so small, Corey," the major said with genuine apprehension.

"Don't worry," said the pilot, "it's just as safe as the big iron ones. You can sit this bird down on a postage stamp if you have to. You're much safer in this little machine than you are in your car any time of the day."

"I believe you," the major said, "but it sure is small."

The pilot looked mildly annoyed for a few moments, then went about preparing the airplane for flight. When he finished looking it over, he attached a tow bar to the nose wheel and tugged the airplane out onto the frozen ramp. He closed the hangar door, jumped on the nonskid walkway at the wing root, opened the plane's door with a pop, and slid across to the left front seat. Corey got into the cramped back seat, and the major rode in the front.

After several grinding turns of the propeller, the engine started with a shudder. The airplane's nose dropped a little, resisting the brakes. The pilot let the engine run for a few minutes, gave several uncomfortable blasts of power to the propeller, and started the small plane moving. It wobbled awkwardly over bumps and ice patches toward the departure end of the runway. Once there, the pilot went through his engine and instrument performance check. Then, as casually as he would have driven his own car, he started rolling the plane down the narrow black strip of runway at full power. The major saw the end of the runway approaching fast, with its wall of white and ice boulders. The tires bumped and thumped on the uneven ground like thin balloons. She closed her eyes, and when she opened them again, she could see only blue sky.

They were up, floating and bouncing on the air above the ground. Cold, winter air flowed around them at a hundred and thirty miles per hour. The major could not read the thermometer—it was twisted toward the pilot—but she knew it was very cold and wondered how thin aluminum metal could stand that sort of punishment.

Most of the land below was still covered with a sugar glaze of icy snow. Trees stood out as gray patches among white frozen water. The major was surprised by the amount of water. Chesapeake Bay was immediately visible and looked like a partially frozen sea into which dirty white fingers of land jutted. They were heading toward one of those fingers.

She glanced over at the pilot, who appeared almost bored, and wondered how she could trust her life to this man. There was only one way down, and he was the only one who knew how to do it. She wished she had not come. She never liked flying, even on large transport category airplanes, and the only advantage the big jets had was that you could easily pretend you were on a bus or a train. And they had restrooms. But this little plane was closer to the essence of flight than she ever wanted to get.

The pilot looked over his shoulder at Corey and pointed to one of the wide peninsulas below. A thin pencil line of black road lay like a twisted string down the middle.

"Does that look like it?" Corey asked, pulling up next to the major's ear.

The major studied the road carefully but didn't see anything she recognized.

"Can you circle and get lower?" Corey asked the pilot.

He answered by reducing the power and lowering the nose of the airplane. The plane seemed to drop like a stone. The major felt her stomach jump with the tingling sensation of a fast elevator ride down. The pilot descended as low as he could go. She recognized the brick gate, but the chain-link fence was difficult to see.

She pointed down and shouted above the roar of the engine, "That's it."

The pilot nodded and made a sharp turn to the left, then back to the right.

"Fly along the fence," Corey said.

The pilot nodded. Corey made a sketch of the place on his road map. There was no visible indication of activity on the property, no plowed fields, no sign of livestock. Most of the grounds were wooded except for the northwest side that bordered a large tributary of the bay. A large pier, extending out into the water, seemed capable of berthing a hundred-foot yacht.

From this perspective, it was clear the house was an H-shaped, two-story structure, and the center section was shorter than the cross sections. There was a formal garden behind the house on the west side, and a large, covered swimming pool on the south side. There were other buildings further to the south at the edge of the wooded area, and a tennis court adjacent to the garden. The road from the highway terminated in a wide, circular drive behind tall gates with a paved parking lot to the side.

"That's the car," the major said, pointing down to a black Lincoln in the driveway. Corey nodded.

They were flying back over the gate again. The pilot looked over his shoulder. "Want me to go round again?" he asked.

"Let's make one turn over the house at a thousand feet so I can see how it sits on the peninsula," Corey said.

The pilot did a sharp right turn and started to climb. The major felt her stomach grow heavy, then a slight rippling pain ran through it. The plane turned steeply over the house. She felt her mouth moisten.

She did not look at the house, fearful it would trigger what she was trying desperately to suppress, and she didn't think she could suppress it for long. She thought of asking the pilot to return as quickly as he could, but she was afraid the slightest move on her part would send the contents of her stomach gushing out—a very undesired outcome.

The pilot leveled the plane, then reached into a side pocket on the door next to him and quickly handed her a plastic-lined bag.

"Just in case you need it," he said with his studied casualness.

She needed it. The major lowered her head into the bag and let go of the agitated substance that was fighting to escape her body. She didn't care about the rest of the flight back to the airport. She just kept her eyes on the clear, thin horizon ahead. She could not have cared if she were over the middle of the ocean, and she was utterly apathetic to the pilot when he missed his first attempt at landing and had to go around for another try. On the second attempt, she watched with indifference as the twisting and bobbing airplane approached the ice wall that marked the end of the runway. The major watched, detached, as it skimmed over the wall, chips of snow blowing off the top. The greatest relief was when the little plane seemed to drop out of the sky and thud against the runway, sounding like an empty metal drum. She breathed deeper as the pilot taxied the plane back to its former position in front of the hangar.

While Corey talked with the pilot and paid the bill, she dumped the plastic bag into a large metal garbage can. Later she met Corey in the office, feeling a resurgence of appetite. He was busy sketching a map of the estate they had just flown over. He wanted to make sure that he had all the entrances and exits from the property noted.

"Sorry about what happened," she said to the pilot.

"Hey, it happens all the time. Don't worry about it."

He handed Corey a receipt and seemed happier now that the office was warm, and he had money in his pocket.

Corey thanked the pilot and they left.

The major asked, "So, what do you think we should do?"

Corey glanced up at her, his eyes intensely serious. "Call the State Police."

"Isn't that kind of risky?"

"It's the only way. You saw the size of the place. Even if I could get into it without being seen, which I don't believe I could do, I would never find him. The police are the only answer. If there is reasonable cause, they can legally search the place, and a kidnapping is reasonable cause."

He caught the major's troubled expression. "Don't worry. They know what to look for. If those thugs have hidden him, there will be something to indicate it. There is always something."

"All right, Corey. I know you're right. Frank wouldn't have had me call you if he didn't have faith in you."

CHAPTER 23

February 24
Saturday, 3:10 p.m.

Frank lay on the soft, ornate bed, unable to sleep. He kept thinking about Mr. Russell, the creator of an important industry, acutely intelligent, forceful in his way, economically powerful, who was now reduced to a state of infancy. It was almost impossible to believe, but Frank couldn't erase the image of Mr. Russell slumped in a wheelchair with his mind of seventy years wiped clean.

And there was Ahmet. At any moment, Frank expected Ahmet to come tearing into the room and start the process of beating him to a pulp. He couldn't let them use their anti-memory drug on Mrs. Rawlson. He would have to tell them about the major and Corey. They, at least, had a chance to fight back. But, if the major had done what she was supposed to do, something should have happened by now. Resigned to somehow achieve the impossible alone, Frank rose from the bed and looked up at the camera.

"All right, I'll tell you what you want to know. But first you have to let Mrs. Rawlson go. She will not be a threat to you. You've got her father."

Frank waited, but there was no answer.

"Hey, are you asleep up there? I said I'll talk!"

He waited, but there was still no answer. He ran to the window.

"Look! I'm gonna go! I'm gonna jump!"

He glanced out of a window and couldn't believe his eyes. A policeman and two state troopers were walking around the south corner of the house. The major had come through! The place was being searched.

He threw open the window and Ahmet suddenly burst into the room, gun drawn, face seized with panic. Frank quickly picked up an antique chair next to him—the one that looked like it had belonged to the Medici family—and held it inches from the window.

"If you shoot," Frank yelled, "you'll bring them up here for sure. You won't have time to get me out of the way, and if the shot doesn't bring them, this chair crashing through the window will. You're up the creek, buddy. That gun is no help to you now."

One of the state troopers was walking slowly, carefully examining the ground along the edge of the building below Frank. In a few minutes he would disappear around the other side. Frank had to do something to goad Ahmet into making a mistake, and fast.

"You see, Ahmet, we Americans aren't as stupid as you think. And when your money runs out, you'll still be what you always were, just a bunch of filthy goat herders."

"You dog! You swine! You infidel!" Ahmet screamed and lunged toward Frank, his gun arm raised like a club. Frank pushed against the chair with all his strength and hurled it through the window. The chair burst outside like it had exploded out of the window. Frank had just enough time to twist to the left and take the impact of his own weight on the wall with his shoulder. Ahmet swung the pistol at his head and missed. The movement threw him off balance, and he hit the floor flat on his back. The gun tumbled in a high arc until it landed in the center of the room. Frank dove for it, grabbing it in both hands, and rolled onto his shoulder up to a standing position. He leveled the gun at

Ahmet's forehead and checked the safety. It was off. The fall had knocked the breath out of Ahmet, and he lay on his back, gasping for air.

Frank ran for the window and shouted, "We're up here! Watch out. They're heavily armed!"

Frank caught a glimpse of the policemen running around the corner of the house. He ran back to the center of the room, took careful aim, and blew the camera lens to pieces. He then turned and held the gun on Ahmet, who had gotten to his feet and was breathing steadily.

"It's over, Ahmet. Your next living quarters will not be as elegant as this."

Ahmet took a few steps toward him. "Perhaps you are wrong," he said.

"One more step, Ahmet, and you'll be on your way to paradise or, in your case, the other place."

Ahmet smiled. "That is good. You are learning courage. I believed that you would. Good! You are an exceptional American."

Ahmet turned and sprinted for the window. Frank watched over the barrel of the pistol as Ahmet dove headfirst through the broken window, hands and feet together like an Olympic high diver. When Frank reached the window, Ahmet was sprawled grotesquely on the frozen ground near the chair and the shattered remnants of window glass, his head twisted around over his shoulder. If Ahmet thought he'd escape, his reckless gamble didn't pay off.

Cautiously, Frank opened the door of the room. The hall was empty. He heard shots in another part of the house. He ran along the hall to the conference room, kicked the door open, and leveled the gun at the table. The room was deserted, the table empty.

There were more shots, closer this time. Frank crouched in the conference room doorway. His best guess was that Mr. Russell and his daughter were somewhere in this hallway. But there must be ten or fifteen rooms in this wing alone.

He heard thudding footsteps approach. He waited. A man ran past the slightly open door of the conference room. It was Shazid.

Frank stepped out into the hall and shouted, "Stop!"

Shazid stopped in his tracks.

"Turn around. Keep your hands out where I can see them."

Shazid turned around. His face was drawn tight with fear and rage.

"Where are they?" Frank demanded.

Shazid's eyes involuntarily flicked to the right.

"Which door?"

Shazid did not move. He wasn't going to make the same mistake again.

"Which door, goddammit!"

Shazid remained unmoved. Frank looked past him at the two doors on the left. He saw Shazid's hand quickly reach behind his back. Frank fired his weapon, and Shazid spun around once and fell onto his face. There wasn't time for remorse. Frank tried the first door, and the room was empty. The same for the second. He proceeded around the corner to a door on the left. He could hear voices. He turned the knob slowly, then pushed it open.

"I was hoping you would drop by, and you did," Saunders said.

He was holding Mrs. Rawlson by her arm and resting the barrel of a 45-caliber pistol against the back of her head. Her eyes were wide with terror. Her father was slumped in the wheelchair a few feet from them.

"Close the door."

Frank did as he was told.

"Lock it."

Frank slid the bolt into place.

"Now drop the gun."

Frank hesitated.

"Drop it!" Saunders screamed.

Frank laid the gun on the floor beside him.

"Over there!" Saunders motioned with the pistol toward Mr. Russell. Frank slowly walked over and stood beside the slumped figure.

"Now we're all going to leave here, except him." Saunders nodded toward Mr. Russell. "And everybody's going to cooperate, or it will be very unpleasant, and people will get killed. Nobody wants that, right?"

There was silence for a few moments. Saunders reached over and opened the window, then pushed Mrs. Rawlson into the opening and fired a shot out of the window. It got the attention of the police.

"Hey! I've got Adams and the old man is here with me too." He pressed the barrel against her temple so that it could be seen from the outside.

A distant voice shouted, "Let the hostages go. There is no way you can escape. Give yourself up and no one will be hurt."

"There's no time for talk," Saunders said. "I want all you cops to get out of the house and stand on the other side of the parking lot. Do it now, or she'll be the first."

There was a long moment of quiet.

"They're doing it," a voice said.

Saunders jerked Mrs. Rawlson away from the window. "Let's give them a few minutes." He then pointed the gun at Mr. Russell's head. Frank realized he fully intended to shoot the man.

"No!" Mrs. Rawlson screamed. "No!"

"Don't do it, Saunders," Frank said. "He can't say anything

against you now. He can't even remember his own name. You might get away with Sal's murder, but you won't be able to get away with this one."

There was a flicker of agreement in Saunders's wild eyes. He lowered the gun, then pressed it against Mrs. Rawlson's head. He looked out the window again and shouted down to the policemen, "Get over there where I can see you all!" He turned to Frank. "Okay, okay, let's go. You try to run for it, Adams, and I'll nail you before you get two feet."

"You've only got so many rounds in that thing," Frank said. He estimated there were four to six rounds left.

"Don't you worry about it. There's enough for you and her."

"And one for yourself?"

"Don't be ridiculous. I fully intend to get out of this alive and claim my riches. Now let's go."

Frank sensed Saunders had crossed the Rubicon and entered a new realm of denial and fantasy. There had been evidence of quirkiness and untrammeled greed during the few times they'd met, but now all the rules were gone, and Saunders was a dangerous madman willing to do anything.

They moved in a tight group of three down the hall and down the circular staircase to a large foyer. Saunders stopped and looked around. He was holding Helen around the neck and Frank stood next to her. The police were lined up on the left side of the parking lot. The household staff had been rounded up and were standing between two police cars. "Move," Saunders snapped, and the trio stepped carefully onto the front porch. Saunders gripped the pistol tighter and pressed it against Mrs. Rawlson's head.

"Get back! Get back!" he shouted at the top of his voice.

The officers stepped back in unison. Frank caught a brief glimpse of the major and Corey in the police line. The temptation to run, to make a quick break for it, was almost overpowering, but that would be a death sentence for Mrs. Rawlson. Several police sharpshooters were stationed on the roof of the house. The police line itself resembled a tightly coiled spring, held in place by a thin wire.

"Let's go," Saunders said in a low voice. They walked slowly toward the black Lincoln. Saunders's eyes darted from side to side. "You drive," he said to Frank. "The keys are in the glove compartment."

Frank got into the driver's seat. The car seemed incongruously luxurious. Upholstered in leather, it bore the aroma of sweet cigars. Saunders edged Mrs. Rawlson into the back seat.

"Start it up and let's go."

"Where?"

"Don't worry about that. Just go. I'll tell you where."

Frank started the car and pulled through the wide-open gates. He could see the police sprinting toward their cruisers in the rearview mirror.

"They're following us," Frank said quietly.

"I expected them to. But there is still nothing they can do." Saunders laughed a deep, nervous, internal laugh that grew into a hysterical bark, then abruptly subsided.

"Where are you going to go, Saunders? You can't expect to get very far. And when the news media get this story, there's no way you're going to get out quietly."

"You just drive and don't worry about what I'm going to do. I've got very important friends. I'll get out of this, and I'll have enough money to buy a small country. As long as I've got Mrs. Rich Bitch and this"—he waved the gun in the air—"I'll make it out of here. You just drive and keep your mouth shut."

Frank noticed a strident tone in Saunders's voice, possibly to cover up for the fact that he didn't quite believe what he was saying. *Maybe he thinks he can bull this through just on the power of the words,* Frank mused, surprised at his own contrasting inner calm. *At least Mr. Russell is no longer in pain,* he thought. Frank glanced in the rearview mirror. Mrs. Rawlson sat rigidly next to Saunders. Her eyes glazed in fear.

After a long silence made even more incongruous by the comfortable purr of the engine, Saunders tapped Frank on the shoulder and said, "It's up here about three miles, a small airport, East Bay Shore Airport, over there to the left. Turn in at the sign. Stop in front of the office door and hand me the keys. Stay in the car until I tell you, then get out and stay in front of me." Saunders got out of the car and dragged Mrs. Rawlson with him. He held the barrel of the gun to her head so the police could easily see it. He shouted at Frank to get out of the car.

Frank had given up on the idea of running. That seemed out of the question now. The police were not far behind. Three police cars, with lights flashing, stopped several hundred feet away. A helicopter was probably on the way.

"Okay, in the office. Hurry!" Saunders demanded.

The pilot was sitting at his desk with his feet resting comfortably on top of it. He was leafing through an aviation magazine. He looked over the top of the magazine and saw Frank, Mrs. Rawlson, then Saunders. His mouth dropped open, then his feet slid off the desktop.

"We're unusually busy today," he observed drily.

"Get up!" Saunders ordered.

The pilot stood up and absentmindedly held on to the aviation magazine.

"Get up!" Saunders ordered again. "Get out maps of southeast Canada."

The pilot stood up quickly. His eyes widened as he noticed

Saunders's gun. "What is this?" he stammered; his bravado gone. He looked at Frank as if expecting a reasonable, logical answer.

"Get to it, creep," Saunders shouted.

"We don't have any charts of Canada," the pilot answered.

"Then get what you have and move!"

The pilot reached into a glass case and fumbled through a stack of folded charts.

"New York. That's it. That's as far north as we go."

"How far north does it cover?"

The pilot unfolded the chart and looked at it. "It covers Pennsylvania, New York State up to the Canadian border, and part of New England."

Saunders ordered Mrs. Rawlson and Frank to lie on the floor, then he jerked the chart out of the pilot's hands and scanned it. "It'll have to do. It'll get us to Buffalo. We can cross there." He folded the chart and stuffed it into his coat pocket. With a deranged smile, he said, "Now, let's all go out to that little plane and take a nice uneventful trip to Buffalo." He glared at the pilot. "Now get the plane fired up!" he seethed.

"I can't do that," the pilot protested. "This plane won't get off the ground with all of us in it and a full load of fuel."

Frank sensed the pilot was stalling for time.

"How much fuel is in it?" Saunders asked.

"Six hours at least with two adults."

"Well, I can't sacrifice that. Adams, you know how to fly one of these things. I know from your file."

"I haven't flown anything in a couple of years."

"Then you'll have to remember, won't you? Get in."

"Saunders, it'll be dark soon." Frank said. "We need to know what the weather is. You can't just jump in an airplane and go, especially at this time of year. And it's particularly bad around the Great Lakes. These little planes aren't designed to fly in all weather."

"Quit complaining, damn it, and get out there and get that airplane ready." He motioned vigorously with the pistol for Mrs. Rawlson to follow Frank.

Frank did a quick preflight inspection of the airplane and did not find anything out of order.

He crawled into the front left seat and buckled his seat belt. Then Saunders climbed into the seat next to Frank who reached across him, closed the door, and latched it. Mrs. Rawlson, in the back seat, seemed to be in a catatonic state. Her pupils, dilated to glossy black, stared straight ahead. Frank followed the plane's checklist carefully, then started the engine. He looked back to the left and saw the pilot running for the police cars as hard as his legs and arms could pump.

Waves of snow dust swirled behind the tail of the plane as Frank started for the runway. Saunders thrust the chart in front of him.

"Do exactly what I tell you!" Saunders said, his voice tense and excited. "And stay low. Fly the ground contours, if necessary, but stay low. I don't want 'em tracking us on radar."

"They won't have to track you, Saunders. The pilot will tell them where you are heading," Frank said.

Saunders laughed. "You continue to underestimate me. We're not going to Buffalo. I have a better place in mind—small, close to the border, underpopulated, and not many cops. We'll cross from there. Canada is a big country with a long, unpatrolled border. Come on, get this thing going. Follow this course." He pointed with the muzzle of his pistol at an irregular line drawn from their position to an airport symbol in northern Vermont.

Frank ran the engine up and checked both magnetos and

engine gauges. "We're ready," he said, looking over at Mrs. Rawlson. Her eyes were closed, and her hands were squeezed together.

They rumbled forward down the runway as Frank applied full power. The course would take them through the most rugged parts of Pennsylvania and New York, all mountains and thinly populated. As the plane gained altitude, they skimmed over the flat Delmarva fields. A farmer, tromping down a muddy path at the edge of his field, looked up casually as they flew over. Frank climbed to seven hundred feet.

"Back down," Saunders ordered.

"I've got to be able to see," Frank snapped. "We're getting close to Wilmington, Delaware. There are thousand-foot towers all around. And if we go over the city, even at this altitude, the police will spot you quicker than they will on radar. Besides, without this"—Frank pointed to the transponder— "it's a very difficult job to track us, even if we were in constant radar contact."

"I know about these things, Adams. I'm an executive for a big avionics firm, remember?" Saunders huffed. "All right," he consented, "but don't go over a thousand feet above ground level, and keep the transponder switched off."

Frank kept Wilmington, Delaware, well off his right wing and crossed the Pennsylvania border northwest of the city and headed across Amish country. He had about a half-hour of daylight left, maybe more, and he needed every second of it. Visibility was deteriorating rapidly. The horizon to the north was black with moisture-laden clouds.

"That's bad weather ahead," Frank said, not faking his ominous tone.

"Just keep going. We've got enough gas to go through it. Keep going."

"But . . ."

"Dammit, shut up and fly the plane. Remember, I'm still in charge here!" Saunders waved the gun threateningly.

The weather, as Frank knew, was the real force in charge. Saunders's gun had no power over what the weather would do to the airplane, and an aircraft was always the obedient subject of weather. He had hoped, even muttered his hope aloud, for snow. With snow, he could keep the plane in the air, but he knew what would happen when the first drops of liquid precipitation hit the windshield and froze there in hard, flat teardrops.

He thought about asking Saunders if he could turn the plane around, but he knew that would be pointless. Maybe this was the best way. Maybe Mother Nature, in all her fury, was the only thing powerful enough to stop Saunders.

Within minutes, enough ice had accumulated on the leading surfaces of the wings to make it feel like a piece of timber blundering through the air.

They began to descend.

"Climb, dammit, climb!" Saunders yelled.

"It's too late now," Frank shouted. "Look at this weather. Why don't you shoot at those clouds up there? Maybe they'll start raining antifreeze if you tell them to. But for now, buddy, we're going down, and it's too late to do anything about it."

"Can't you turn on the deicer or something?"

"This aircraft does not have deicing capability."

Frank slipped the plane between two rows of white hills whiskered with naked gray trees. There were some clearings in the valley, as he had hoped. However, the only one he could possibly make looked like a small patch of blurred white.

He glanced over at Mrs. Rawlson and told her to tighten her seat belt and shoulder harness before tightening his own. Just before crossing a frozen hedgerow, he turned off all electrical switches and the fuel selector and unlatched the cabin door so that it popped open slightly. As the touchdown spot approached, and estimating his height above it, Frank tried with all the strength he had left to raise the nose of the airplane. It responded slowly and sluggishly. At that moment, the airplane thudded on to the frozen ground, throwing up waves of snow and ice.

He could hear the crunching sounds of tearing metal and felt a force throwing him violently to the left. He heard Mrs. Rawlson scream, then darkness.

Frank gradually became aware that someone was shaking him. At first, he thought he might be on the warm palm-lined coast of a tropical resort, that he was being awakened from a bad dream by the beautiful girl he had met in the hotel bar the day before. But it was a dream, of course. The beach sand turned out to be snow, and the beautiful girl became Helen Rawlson's terrified face, demanding tearfully that he return to the living.

Frank felt the tender spot on his head. It felt like a bruised apple, but it was still too numb to hurt badly.

"Did you get the gun?" he asked.

"I couldn't find it. It must have been thrown outside when we hit the ground."

The door was twisted open, and snow and ice pellets were blowing in. The left window was cracked, probably where he hit his head.

"Are you all right?" Frank asked.

"Yes. What do we do now?"

Frank released his seat belt. Saunders appeared to be unconscious.

"Let's get him out of here and look for something to tie him up. Look in the baggage compartment."

Frank eased himself out onto the bent wing and reached in for Saunders. Unexpectedly, there was a gun in his face.

"No, you don't," Saunders said, his voice hoarse and strained.

Impulsively, almost as soon as he saw the gun, Frank slammed the door. He heard the gun clatter against it and felt the soft thud of Saunders's head on the plexiglass. He opened the door again but couldn't see the gun. He grabbed Mrs. Rawlson by the arm and started pulling her with him. She didn't protest as they leapt off the wing into knee-deep snow.

"Let's get away from the plane," Frank said.

"We're not dressed for this! How long can we last out here?" Mrs. Rawlson asked.

"We need to get away from Saunders. We'll find some shelter. I'm sure choppers can't be far behind."

"Can helicopters fly in this weather?"

"Some rescue helicopters have a thermo-electric system that can heat the rotors. I'm hoping the police have that equipment. But most choppers can't fly in icing conditions. We can only keep our fingers crossed."

They fought against the hard crust of ice that had formed on top of the snow. They ran like waders in knee-deep water, occasionally tripping on some submerged object and falling headfirst into the crusty snow. They picked themselves up and hopped and danced over the snow until Frank felt the ground beneath him disappear. They both tumbled forward, rolling like logs down the long side of a ditch, coming to a rest at the bottom.

Frank saw something—a crude structure a few yards down the ditch. From this distance, it looked like the opening of a tunnel.

"Let's head in that direction," Frank said through chattering teeth.

They struggled through the snow drifts toward the structure. As they approached, they discovered it to be a small cavity created by several fallen trees across the ditch, which was covered in hardpacked snow. They hacked the opening a bit wider, crawled in, and stomped on the layer of snow and ice that covered the floor of their cave. Frank and Mrs. Rawlson huddled together for warmth.

"We just need . . . to wait. We . . . will be okay," Frank said, shivering.

They heard a shot ring out, echoing in the silence. Then Saunders's distant voice demanded they show themselves. There was another shot, and it was quiet for a while until they heard Saunders's heavy footsteps crunching through the snow, breaking twigs and rotten branches underfoot.

"Stay calm," Frank whispered.

They heard Saunders walk close to their little shelter. He stopped briefly, then walked on out of earshot. It was too dark to see the disturbances in the snow Frank and Mrs. Rawlson had made. Frank could still hear Saunders' footsteps crunching in the snow. Saunders stopped for a moment, listening for human sounds, and when he didn't hear any, he moved on, stumbling his way through the snow, trees, and darkness.

Frank and Mrs. Rawlson waited, huddled closer, and shivered in what little warmth their bodies provided, not speaking, thinking only of warmth and the morning. After about an hour, when Frank was reasonably sure that Saunders had wandered far enough away, he cautioned Mrs. Rawlson to stay put and pulled himself out of the snow cave. Crouching low, he prowled his way to the wrecked airplane.

Frank's silent wish had come true: the airplane's emergency locator beacon had deployed automatically, just as it was designed to do. It emitted loud, desperate beeps over the emergency frequency, guiding the police helicopter over the hills to this narrow valley.

Right on cue, a helicopter, flying low and flashing its search lights, circled the wreckage once and then settled in next to it in a swirling cloud of ascending snow. Frank felt the strength go out of his legs as he collapsed next to the wreckage.

Two men wearing blue police fatigue uniforms, and holding rifles leapt from the helicopter and moved cautiously toward the wrecked plane.

"Over here!" Frank yelled. "Over here!"

Both men turned toward the sound of his voice. Then one of them ran toward him, fighting his way through the snow, swinging his rifle like a supporting counterweight.

The policeman arrived, looking serious and doubtful. Frank gave him his name and led him to Mrs. Rawlson. The policeman looked at her, then called the helicopter pilot with his hand radio. Moments later, two more men arrived bearing blankets and a rescue basket. They bundled Mrs. Rawlson up like a tortilla and secured her in the litter. Frank wrapped himself in a blanket. Still feeling very weak, he was assisted into the chopper.

On the way back, as Frank marveled at the tangle of nets, ropes, cages, and other Search and Rescue equipment, a man with a clipboard shouted questions at Frank. Another spoke on the radio and conferred with the pilot, and a third was attending to Mrs. Rawlson. They offered Frank a hot drink. He sipped it slowly, shuddered with new warmth, and watched them attend to Mrs. Rawlson.

They relayed to Frank that Saunders had been found a few hundred feet away from the wreckage and had been led away in handcuffs to a second chopper.

"He's alive?" Frank asked.

"Yes, but I don't know how," the officer said. "If anybody else had spent that much time exposed to the elements the way he was, they would have turned to a block of ice."

"Adrenaline helps you endure anything," Frank said.

"And don't forget hope, sir," the officer said. "Hope can keep you alive for a long time."

CHAPTER 24

March 1996

Frank stood at the front door of the Rawlson estate, enjoying the profusion of bright yellow daffodils flanking the large stone porch. A neatly dressed maid answered the door. Frank introduced himself. The maid smiled warmly and invited him in. He followed her into the foyer.

"I'll tell Mrs. Rawlson that you're here."

Frank nodded politely. It seemed like years since he had been in this beautiful house. It didn't seem as light and airy then. He had the feeling that the house itself had thrown off a great burden and was joyously happy to be free of it.

The original lab reports and the brokerage receipts were more than enough to convict Saunders of fraud. He confessed to being complicit in Charles Rawlson's murder, and he was sentenced to fifty years. Frank would consider that a win.

Helen Rawlson entered the foyer from the rear left, a room Frank had never been in.

"So glad you could come," she said. She sounded calm and rested. She held an envelope in her hand. "I meant to send this by mail, but I wanted to see you again and thank you for everything. You saved my life in more ways than one, and you tried to save my father's too."

"It's a shame he died, but in a way—"

"Yes, in his condition, it was a blessing." she said. She handed him the envelope. "It was a terrible thing. He was the only member of my family left. I'll have to find a way to go on. My father would not want me to give up. That's not a family trait."

"Will you be taking over the company?" Frank asked.

She smiled. "Thank you for everything, Frank. Keeping those original documents separate in the company safe was brilliant!"

Frank smiled, pleased with her gratitude.

Her eyes became distant. "The papers say that Saunders will probably not live long enough to be eligible for parole."

"I read that too, but you can't believe anything you read in the papers."

"You know, Frank, when I was in the hospital, I just wished that he would die. I wished to God that he would die. But now I don't feel that way anymore. I just want to get on with my life and make the business even better than it was. The company is sixty precent mine now. There is no one else, but in my mind and heart, it's still a family-owned company. And it's not as new to me as I thought. I must have absorbed more than I realized. It's going to be a wonderful challenge. I feel totally confident."

"Good. You'll do all right. You've still got everything to live for. And your father would be very proud."

"I know. And I think he knows too."

They smiled warmly; the way people do when they look back with sympathy on the past. She slid her arm through his and walked him to the door.

"Please come back anytime," she said. She kissed him lightly on the cheek, then walked away.

"And never forget!" he called after her.

She turned and looked at him with a quizzical smile.

"Daffodils always bloom in March!"

Frank skipped quickly down the wide brick path to Pedro's waiting taxi.

"Let's go, Pedro," he said, and he slipped into the back seat.

He opened the envelope. There was a check for $25,000 and ten shares of Amertek Electronics, Inc.

"Hot damn! This means a good, long time in Baja, Pedro."

The major was standing next to her luggage in the lobby of her condo when Frank and Pedro arrived.

"Can you go?" Frank asked.

"I told 'em that I wanted to use my twenty days of sick leave for mental health reasons."

"Did you have to show them a note from the doctor?"

The major laughed. "Nope, they understood because they all need twenty days of mental health leave themselves."

They burst into laughter, then they managed to stack all her bags in the trunk of the cab, leaving only a small overnight case in the front seat with Pedro.

"Let's go," Frank said. "Pedro, take a long, hot road across the desert. It may be July before we get to Baja."

"I hope so," the major said.

ABOUT THE AUTHOR

A retired FAA Aviation Safety Inspector, Daniel V. Meier, Jr. has always had a passion for writing. He studied history at the University of North Carolina, Wilmington (UNCW), and American literature at the University of Maryland Graduate School.

Meier also worked as a journalist for the *Washington Business Journal* and is a contributing writer/editor for several aviation magazines. *Guidance to Death* is a return to action/thriller, his favorite genre, with the added intrigue of murder and mystery.

Other books by Meier are *Blood Before Dawn*, the sequel to the award-winning novel, *The Dung Beetles of Liberia*. His other works include *Bloodroot*, a historical novel about the Jamestown settlement in the early 1600s, and *No Birds Sing Here*, a work of satirical literary fiction. In 1980, he published an action/thriller, *Mendosa's Treasure*, with Leisure Books under the pen name of Vince Daniels.

Meier and his wife live in Owings, Maryland, about twenty miles south of Annapolis, and when he's not writing, they spend their summers sailing on the Chesapeake Bay.